NANNY WITH BENEFITS

A SINGLE DAD & NANNY ROMANCE

MICHELL LOVE

CONTENTS

Sign Up to Receive Free Books	v
1. Jayce	1
2. Leila	9
3. Jayce	18
4. Leila	26
5. Jayce	34
6. Leila	42
7. Jayce	50
8. Leila	58
9. Jayce	65
10. Leila	73
11. Jayce	80
Exile: A Single Father & A Virgin Romance	91
Untitled	117
About the Author	119

Made in "The United States" by:

Michelle Love

© Copyright 2020 – Michelle Love

ISBN: 978-1-64808-399-0

ALL RIGHTS RESERVED. No part of this publication may be reproduced or transmitted in any form whatsoever, electronic, or mechanical, including photocopying, recording, or by any informational storage or retrieval system without express written, dated and signed permission from the author

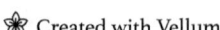 Created with Vellum

SIGN UP TO RECEIVE FREE BOOKS

Sign Up to Receive Free E-Books and Audiobook Codes.

Would you like to read **The Unexpected Nanny, Dirty Little Virgin** and **other romance books** for **free**?

You can sign up to receive these free e-books and audiobooks by typing this link into your browser:

https://www.steamyromance.info/free-books-and-audiobooks-hot-and-steamy/

Or this one:

https://www.steamyromance.info/the-unexpected-nanny-free/

BLURB

"My life was finally where I wanted it to be ... or was it?"

The price was my family, my hometown, and my reputation but my musical career was finally panning out. Unfortunately, the universe had other plans for my brother and me, taking me back from LA to Alpena, Michigan.
I would not have gotten far without Leila Butler, my brother Micah making no secret how he loathed me. If it wasn't for the sexy, sweet blonde and her amazing way with him, who knew where I'd be?
Probably back in LA where I belonged.

"I'd held onto my virginity long enough to lose it to the most unlikely candidate—a wander-lusting bad boy with no desire to stay put."

And I knew better too. Everyone knew that Jayce Joyce was selfish—he left his family behind, hoping to find himself in Los Angeles.
Had he always been this gorgeous? Maybe I was starstruck. Was that why I couldn't decline when he offered me a job watching over the house and Micah?
I really wanted to watch over him.
Yet, right from the start, I knew his heart didn't really belong to me—the music was claiming him again, just as it had before. How could a small-time girl like me compete with the glitz and glamour of LA?

Jayce

When I was about four or five, I remember telling my dad I wanted a little brother. Even then, he looked at me with hauntingly chocolate eyes and shook his head like I had asked him for both of his kidneys.
"It's not in the cards, Jason," he declared in the same tone he used when I asked for another serving of ice cream for dessert. "Just not in the cards."
It took me a few years to understand why he looked at me like that—the fact he and my mom were teenagers when they had me and my request had come when he was a twenty-one-year-old high school dropout, working for pennies as a farmhand while my mom cleaned hotel rooms in our little town of Alpena, Michigan.
Reflecting back on those years, I don't remember having a need—there was always food on the table, even if it was KD three nights out of seven. I had my own room as well, even if it was the size of the walk-in closet at my place in Los Angeles. It actually may have been smaller—I never measured. In retrospect, having to share that space was not pleasant for anyone—four people in a two-bedroom trailer wasn't exactly opulence. Three people were bad enough. Not that I had a concept of what the high life was back then.
It didn't help that I was not the most obedient child, a trait that didn't improve with maturity. I guess it took a couple of decades for the bitter memory of raising me to wear off before they tried again.
Too bad my parents didn't anticipate they could possibly have a worse kid than me, especially not in their forties. Or maybe it

was better they were older—they say the older you get, the less you care. I never found that to be true. Of course, I wasn't in my forties.

Nevertheless, Micah was a bigger shithead than I ever was, even if I say so myself.

I was thinking of this as I smirked at my parents. Sitting in my spot across from my younger brother, I was watching his abhorrent table manners with my peripheral vision. I would never have gotten away with that when I was his age. Dad would have given me a single backhand to the head and I would have sat up and used my knife. Or even just "the look." Whatever happened to "the look"? Kids nowadays get away with murder. "Just because we're poor, Jason, doesn't mean you have to act like an animal!" Dad would chant in my ear so much, I would hear it in my dreams. I guess the same rules didn't apply for Micah.

There was a decided contrast in the dining room that night. Mom had gone all out again, decorating for the season, the fading white string lights and low-playing Christmas tunes in the background, the seven-foot real pine emanating an overpowering aroma as it sparkled with glass bulbs and tinsel garlands. Presents were already all over the floor even though the 25th was two days away. None of that, not even the crackling wood of the fireplace in the living room, could overpower the unspoken tension looming over our small family, sucking the air from the room.

"So, Jason, honey," my mom, Beth, cooed in her soft, maternal way. "How's the singing?"

My half smile quickly faded; my eyes darting toward her scowling.

"My singing?" I echoed in disbelief. "How's my singing?"

It never ceased to amaze me how easily disdain arose.

"Watch your tone, Jason," Dad snapped without looking up

from his roast beef. He was on autopilot, ready to verbally reprimand me like in childhood.

Oh sure, but you can't see your youngest shoveling peas into his mouth like a zombie apocalypse is at the door, right?

"I'm sorry, baby," Mom sighed. "Did I offend you?"

She sounded exhausted; no surprise. Things had gotten decidedly better for my parents, specifically after I'd moved from Michigan and pursued my career in Los Angeles. Gone was the shitty trailer in Greenhaven Community Park. I didn't know how that hunk of metal had survived as long as it had. Nowadays my parents lived in a quaint two-story abode on the outskirts of Alpena. Dad wasn't toiling on someone else's farm, not since the app he'd developed went viral. Who knew people could make money creating apps? But Mom? She seemed tired, despite the fact she hadn't worked since Micah was born. Handling that kid was worse than cleaning toilets. Or maybe she was weary of life. My dad was a prick sometimes. Since childhood, I hadn't been able to imagine why she'd married him.

This was the first time I had been home in three years and it was already regretful, even though, admittedly, eating Mom's concoctions was better than I remembered. Between recording sessions, I didn't get a lot of pot roast at all.

"My singing is great, Mom," I grunted, tossing my fork on the table and running a hand through my wavy black hair. It was getting long, but my agent, Daryn, told me to leave it, that women loved the "rock-star" look. Yup, her name was Daryn, but in LA everyone was graced with ridiculous names, I had quickly learned. I had no idea what was their birthright and which were monikers and had stopped asking long ago.

"Don't you have a song or something?" Micah piped up, his mouth bursting with potatoes.

"Micah," Mom chided tenderly. "Don't speak with your mouth full."

My brother ignored her and kept his dark eyes focused on me. He looked like Dad, like us. We all had the same jet-black hair and intense brown eyes. My poor mom's recessive blonde genes didn't stand a chance. Dad had told me once that there was native blood four generations back or something. I'd always maintained the school of thought that we were all mixed with something after thousands of years of war, but that's another story.

"Well? Don't you?" Micah insisted, and it annoyed me. I might have been a brat, but never that rude. Meaningfully, I looked at my father, wondering if he would rein in his youngest, but he seemed oblivious.

The baby really gets away with everything!

"I have a few songs," I retorted. "My latest single is climbing the charts."

I told my family about my success. Leaving Alpena had been the best decision—there was absolutely nothing for me in that one-horse town. Although I should have done it sooner.

"Yeah. I think one of my teachers likes your music," Micah said, turning his attention back to his meal. It stung me that my own brother didn't care if I made it huge in the music industry. Against all odds, a poor-ass kid from Nowhere, Michigan, had made his way into the daunting world of rock and here was my punk-ass brother, making me feel like a nobody.

I shouldn't have come home, Christmas or not. I shouldn't have succumbed to my mom's wistful emails and guilt trips. They'd asked me to visit to make me feel like shit.

And they'd succeeded. Again.

"That's wonderful, honey," Mom said, likely sensing my rising frustration. "I'll have to pick up your CD."

Micah and I both guffawed.

"CD?" we chorused, exchanging a look. Mom looked embarrassed.

"Isn't that how we listen to music?"

Micah giggled, and I couldn't help but grin at her dated views but simultaneously gave her credit for making an effort. My dad had barely uttered a coherent sentence since I'd arrived the previous day. He was still pissed about my going off on my own shortly after Micah was born, and he was not proud of my choices.

I was waiting for the lid on his top to blow.

"So that's it?" Dad said suddenly, raising his head for the first time. "You'll continue to chase this juvenile fantasy?"

My back stiffened.

There it is. It didn't take him long.

"Gary ..." Mom gave my father a warning look but it was too late. He was there. To his credit, he probably had held out as long as he could.

"Fantasy? Making six figures a year is not a fantasy."

Dad stared at me, the contempt on his face unmasked. It was hard to believe we were only seventeen years apart. He was like an old man to me, even in adulthood, even at the age of thirty. In LA, I had friends his age but they were nothing like this judgmental, glowering bear that looked at me as if he'd caught me skipping class.

No matter how successful I become, I'll always be the same kid to him.

"And what? You're going to be like Keith Richards?" he insisted, disdain in his voice. "Is that what you think? You'll play rock and roll until you're dead?"

That's ridiculous. Keith Richards will never die. He's a vampire or something.

"GARY!"

"What, Beth? He's thirty years old. He's chased this stupid dream long enough. It's one thing to encourage his creativity and quite another to guide him into homelessness."

"You're homeless?" Micah asked, his eyes widening. "Cool!"

"NOT COOL!" both my parents yelled in unison.

I rose from the table, steeling my shaking hands. It always caught me off guard when he confronted me like that. I loathed myself for letting him getting under my skin again. That was why I'd stayed away for so long.

"Thanks for dinner, Mom." I coldly tossed my napkin on the table. "I'm going to bed and leaving in the morning."

I didn't give her a chance to respond and stormed away from the table.

"JASON!" she cried after me. "Gary! Go after him. It's Christmas, for God's sake! He hasn't been home in years!"

But it wouldn't matter what he said. Even if he apologized, he thought I was a failure. It didn't matter that I was so close to a contract with a real label. He'd scoff and ask how many times he'd heard that before.

I wasn't sitting through it. I'd come too far, struggled too hard to be mocked by my own family.

Falling on the bed in the guest bedroom (which had once been my room for a brief time) I stared at the ceiling and tried to steady my nerves.

I'll catch the first flight back to LA and won't come back until he's dead.

The thought shamed me but before I could justify it, there was a knock at the door.

"I don't want to hear it!" The door opened anyhow and Micah appeared.

"Are you really leaving tomorrow?" he asked from the threshold.

He'd traded his dinner for a piece of chocolate cake which he stabbed with a fork as he spoke. Life continued when I was gone.

No one batted an eye. They just pulled out the cake. Maybe that's why they pulled out the cake—in celebration.

"Yep." More guilt. It wasn't Micah's fault I was angry. He might have a little snot, but he was only six years old and I didn't know him at all. Thanks to Dad, my brother was a stranger to me.

"You can come visit me in LA," I told him, softening my tone. "I'm sure Mom would bring you."

His eyebrows shot up as he chewed on his cake deliberately, watching me with curious eyes. It took him a long while to swallow.

"Why?" he finally asked.

"Why what? There's tons to do."

"Why would I come and visit you?"

I felt heat warming my cheeks.

"Why not? We're brothers, you know."

Micah shrugged.

"I guess." He stuffed another forkful of icing into his mouth. This time he didn't wait until his mouth was clear before speaking. "I don't really know you."

My neck was so tense it was going to snap.

"We could change that. We could hang out and ... stuff."

That sounded so lame but I didn't know how to talk to this kid. He was absolutely correct. We shared blood, but that was it. And if I don't make an effort, that's all we'll ever be—strangers who share blood.

"What do you say?" I pressed when he didn't respond. "Will you come visit?"

He shook his head.

"I don't think so," he replied, turning away.

"Wait! Why not?"

He glanced at me and sighed.

"Because things are ... heavy. You make things ... I dunno ... harder."

He was gone, leaving me processing what he said.

A full-grown man had been dismissed by a six-year-old and reprimanded by his father.

I sat up and began packing my suitcase, determined to leave tonight. I didn't need this. I was just fine in California without them.

Why did I suppose having a brother was a good idea? I gritted my teeth.

I called a cab and proceeded to Alpena County Regional Airport with only one phrase ringing in my mind with sheer resolve.

It will be too soon if I see them again. I don't need them.

And I meant it ... at the time.

1

JAYCE

In the recording studio, the headphones canceled out the sounds around me as I poured my soul into the microphone, my eyes firmly closed. I was caught up in the melody flowing from my lips and into the track.

It was the same when I finished a song I'd sweated over; the all-nighters perfecting the lyrics, the bickering with bandmates, self-deprecation—all worthwhile. I wasn't there—I was a lover calling back his long-gone woman, a jilted groom or a rebel, giving the finger to the establishment. I was whatever the song directed me to be.

That was why I didn't realize the engineer was tapping on the glass, waving his hands and desperately trying to get my attention. The music stopped, but I never used it as a guide—it was easier to sing from the heart. Until a hand was on my shoulder, I was soloing for a full minute. It was not recorded.

"What the feck?" I snapped. "This is the best take yet!"

Jerome shook his shaggy blond head apologetically.

"Sorry, man," the sound engineer sighed. "Your time is up. Axion P and his crew have the space."

Indignantly, I glowered at him.

It was a minute after eleven. One damn minute.

"Seriously?" I spat. "He couldn't wait ten minutes?"

"He booked the space," Jerome reminded me. "And you were running over time."

I was incensed. The rapper was never on time for anything, including his concerts. I highly doubted that Axion was there. Jerome was just covering his own ass in case the infamous hip-hop artist showed his face early. God forbid he had to wait.

"Sorry, man," Jerome said again, and I almost believed him.

You will be sorry, I thought, tossing the headphones from around my neck. One day soon, I'd be the one who made the studio staff jump for me. The following day, I had a meeting scheduled with Sony.

After almost a decade of working my tail to the bone, playing shitholes in Vegas and recording in garages, at last, I was getting a record deal.

I didn't bother to share this information with Jerome. That'd be right before he was informed we would no longer record with Muse Studios.

It'll be worth the look on his face. Even though I'd miss the place. It had its charms, and it had been a home away from my eclectic Santa Monica home.

"Whatever, man." Fearful of slipping the good news, I did not engage. I was known to unload data at inappropriate times.

I grabbed my electric guitar and packed it, careful not to catch my fingers in the heavy casing before locking it.

"You can leave that, man," Jerome said, sounding alarmed when he realized I was taking it with me. "You're back tomorrow, right?"

"Maybe."

I didn't bother to look at him, stalked toward the door, and moved down the halls of Muse, fuming.

There was no sign of Axion or his crew.

Such bullshit.

"You gonna punch something?" a voice chirped when I jabbed the down button for the elevator. I grimaced, seeing who it was.

You would know what I look like when I'm ready to clock something, The day was getting worse by the minute and it wasn't even noon. I should have looked both ways before leaving the sound booth. Miguel was always lurking around.

It's just one more reason to get the hell out of Muse. Good riddance to all you assholes.

"Probably," I conceded. "Are you offering your face?"

Miguel snickered and cast a sidelong look as he approached. Thankfully, I still made him uncomfortable.

"I caught your vocals earlier. You're sounding really good, Jayce. This album will be your best."

Sony thinks so.

"Thanks."

Damn, it was hard to be civil to that prick.

The stainless-steel doors opened and we stepped onto the lift. Miguel punched the lobby button as we stood in silence. It was strained, undoubtedly. Life was different in LA than the rest of the country. Things regarded as taboo to ordinary folk were commonplace behavior to Los Angelinos.

Things like your bandmates screwing your girlfriend.

Miguel, the bassist in my band, had been the first person I'd really bonded with in LA. Unfortunately for me, Teresa, my girlfriend of six months, had bonded with him too. Miguel had decided, "for the sake of the band," that he should seek other ventures after their fling had come to light, but I saw him in the studio more often than was agreeable.

There hadn't even been an apology; neither from Teresa nor Miguel, like I was overreacting and better grow thicker skin to make it in the cutthroat world I'd chosen.

Who knew? Maybe they were right. They had taught me a valuable lesson about trust and how not to have any.

As a result, I played nice with Miguel but couldn't help but distrust all the other bandmates too. Who else Teresa had been with? I mean, she'd sworn it was only once, and only with Miguel, but I didn't believe her, not when Miguel looked at me like he knew something I didn't.

Or maybe I was paranoid. LA had a way of making people loopy.

The doors slid open and I shoved past Miguel before he could move, a fleeting sense of satisfaction that I made it out first, but I realized how stupid it was to feel smug about something so petty.

If you're going to feel cocky about something, feel cocky about your meeting tomorrow. Nothing can destroy that feeling, It was a crisp morning. Thanksgiving was just around the corner and the air had a slight chill. Overhead, rain clouds slowly began to form over the valley in a depressing gray, and I idly wished I had a sweater. I grabbed my key fob and unlocked the 2014 Audi I'd bought a couple years back; my closest thing to a new car. I reminded myself I'd be getting a BMW any day ... as soon as that deal was signed.

Before backing out of my spot, I gazed at the studio—a steel structure with no warmth or personality. There had been three other studios before Muse and were bound to be dozens after.

Dozens. I am setting my sights high ...

Nothing wrong with that. I wouldn't be here if I didn't.

I peeled out of my spot like I intended to leave the place in the figurative dust, winding out of the city traffic toward my place near Palisades Park. At this hour of the morning there was not much transit but still, it was the city. My cell rang during this stop and go. I took it on my Bluetooth.

"Daryn," I laughed. "Talk to me."

"There he is!" my agent cooed through the speakers. "My rising star!"

That phrase made me cringe. I didn't particularly care for the reminder I hadn't fully risen.

"Are you guys ready for the meeting with Sony tomorrow?" Daryn asked, and I chuckled.

"Is anyone ever ready for something like that?" I replied. "Of course not."

"Good! Show them your sweet, humble side, Jayce. They love thinking they can mold you."

"You mean manipulate," I countered sardonically.

"Tsk, tsk, now don't be like that, Jayce. This is what we've been working toward. Your bandmates are anxious. You could stand to be a little more grateful."

If she could see the way my stomach was flipping, we wouldn't be having this conversation, but alas, all she saw was my cynical exterior.

"I am eternally grateful for all you've done," I told her sincerely. "Sony at 9:00."

"Oh no," she purred, her voice filling my ears from every section of the vehicle. "I have a surprise for you. Make sure you're there at 8:30."

"I don't like surprises." An image of Teresa popped into my head.

"I don't care."

I should have expected this from her. Daryn was not a woman to be argued with and I certainly would not fight her on something as trivial as a nice gesture.

"8:30 it is. Anything else?"

"Bring a nice pen. You'll want to remember the moment you signed the biggest deal of your life."

I chortled. "All right, Daryn."

"Toodles."

She disconnected the call, leaving me grinning. We really did owe Daryn a great deal. The success of our band, Rune, would have been limited to back-alley bars and opener shows without her.

She was a shark and well-known in the industry. Being on her roster was the next best thing to being coupled with Daniel Lanois.

And one day, maybe we'll be as big as U2.

She instinctively knew how to boost our image, what gigs to set up for us, our name. It was because of Daryn Jameson that I had gone from Jason Jensen to Jayce Joyce.

"I love the way it just rolls off the tongue," she'd said to me. "It's sexy, and sexy sells. No matter how talented you are, Jayce—and make no mistake, you are talented—it doesn't matter if your fans don't want to be bent over a table."

Sometimes I thought of bending Daryn over a table but suspected she'd own me if that situation ever arose. And I was most certainly not one to be on the bottom.

I steered the car into the carport and grabbed my guitar, locking the door before jogging up the front entrance. My bad mood completely diminished after speaking with Daryn even though fat drops of rain began to splatter against the pavement when I let myself in.

The sun was entirely blotted out and inside my small but awesome home, it was unusually dark for so early in the day.

I flipped on a few lights before plopping onto the couch, draping my legs atop the overstuffed cushions. My cell had six texts and I already knew without looking that they were from the band. The guys were deliriously happy about the future and who could blame them? We'd arrived where we'd aspired to be.

I stared at the phone for a long moment and got an overwhelming desire to call Mom. Ever since Sony had arranged for this meeting three weeks earlier, I'd wrestled with the same demon every time I was alone. I wanted to tell her the good news, but it wasn't to spread the joy—only so that she would tell my jerk father my "childish fantasy" would gross me more than he'd ever seen in his life.

Perhaps that wasn't true—I wasn't sure how much Sony was offering, but it had to be substantial.

It burned me that, after four years, I was still angry with my father, even though he'd acted as he always had, looking down on me like I wasn't worthy of the fame I'd worked so hard to reach.

I hadn't spoken to him since that Christmas and the relationship with my mom wasn't good either. When we did, she would force Micah on the phone but those conversations were short and awkward.

I tossed the cell aside before my fingers took over without my mind agreeing. Maybe I'd wait to give Mom an actual figure on our advance before making the call.

I was growing heavy-eyed. The rain always did that to me, creating a haze which made me want to nap.

At first I fought it, thinking about things to do today, but then I shoved the list aside and embraced the idea of a siesta. I'd earned it.

My lids barely closed before I was caught in a bizarre dream. I didn't remember a great deal but I saw my mom shaking her head at me. She kept repeating something before pointing over my shoulder. When I turned, Micah was staring at me with a blank expression on his face. He looked older and ... scared.

I pivoted back but my mother was gone and my dad was standing there, his face covered in blood.

That was enough to spring me awake. At the same time, I realized it wasn't the only thing which had woken me—my cell was ringing too.

A full storm had taken hold while I napped, the wind

picking up, the branches of the orange trees swinging wildly against the almost-black sky.

"Hello?" I mumbled, clearing my throat after the fact. If I'd looked at the call display, I would have seen it was a private number—not that it would have stopped me from answering it.

"Jason Jensen?"

I blinked several times, pulling the phone back to look at the caller. It told me nothing. It was weird to be called "Jason" after legally changing my name to Jayce Joyce many years ago. Nothing good would come from this call.

"Who is this?"

"Is this Jason Jenson?" the man sounded stern, authoritative, and my first thought was the IRS.

Outside, thunder rumbled and my jaw locked as I debated whether to tell him it was me.

"This is Detective Blake Corso of the Alpena Police Department. Is this Jason Jensen?"

A flash of lightning streaked the sky outside my living room window and I froze, knowing the horrific foreshadowing that only occurred in movies. My dream came flooding back to me full force and a sick feeling rocked my gut.

This wasn't a bad movie—it was my life, no matter how much of it seemed to play in slow motion.

"Yeah," I finally rasped. "This is he."

"Mr. Jensen, I'm afraid I have some bad news for you."

He didn't need to finish his thought. I already knew what he was going to say.

One of my parents had died.

2

LEILA

Bad news always spreads through small towns like wildfire, and this instance was no different.

Sitting in Rosalie's Diner, having my morning coffee, all anyone could talk about was the horrible car accident from the night before and I wished they would stop. It gave me shivers every time I thought about it and it seemed that was all I could think about.

"He was drunk as a skunk," Sarah Millerson sighed, pouring from a pitcher as she shook her head. "Driving the wrong way on the freeway."

"It's a goddamn shame the driver in the semi survived," Pat Richards grunted. "That bastard should rot in hell."

"I'm sure he's in his own kind of hell this morning," Sarah replied softly, shooting me a look across the counter. "Imagine waking up and learning you killed someone. That's a hangover you'll never recover from."

"Killed someone?" Pat scoffed. "He did a lot more than that! He's a murdering son of a bitch. I hear his room at the hospital is under guard. Our tax dollars at work, huh? Protecting a piece of shit like that. I tell you, if he wasn't guarded, I'd go down there and get my own form of justice on that asshole, you know what I mean?"

I wanted to scream at him to stop it, my heart thudding madly as Pat grew more incensed. Sitting back, turning my eyes away from Pat's reddening face, I bit on my lower lip. Tears were burning behind my blue eyes but I willed myself not to cry.

I knew the Jensens, had even babysat Micah a few times over the years, which made the tragedy all the more real, but my heart was just as broken for the driver of that truck, drunk or not. I couldn't imagine what that man was going through.

It's easy for Pat to judge the man but I've seen him get behind the wheel after having a six-pack or more. It could just as easily have been Pat who made that fatal mistake.

Of course, these were not things I said aloud. I wasn't looking for a fight—not then and not ever. Leila Butler wasn't known for speaking her mind. I was more known for my quiet manner, a tender smile, and keeping the peace.

Except there was nothing peaceful about Rosalie's this morning, and the negativity was overwhelming.

"More coffee, hon?"

Sarah appeared before me, coffee jug in her weathered hands.

"No. Just the check, Sarah."

She nodded, casting me a final, worried gaze, and headed for the till. I grabbed my jacket from the neighboring stool and threw it over my shoulders.

"See ya, Leila!" Pat called after me, but I only waved at him without turning So he didn't see my expression. I wasn't much known for my poker face, something Sarah noticed when I stood by the register to pay.

"You shouldn't take these things to heart, hon," Sarah mentioned softly when I handed her a ten-dollar bill. "There is nothing you can do about it."

"Doesn't make it any less heartbreaking," I muttered. "Keep the change."

She yelled out a thank-you but I was already out the door and halfway to my Jeep. I was pushing it for time, having spent too much of my morning eavesdropping on the regulars as they talked about the accident.

Accident. What a pathetic word for what happened. The whole thing could have been avoided with a little foresight.

I was far too distracted to drive and when I pulled up in the employee lot, I was glad I'd made it in one piece. I hoped the conversation at work wouldn't be the accident but the upcoming day didn't give me a good feeling. Turned out, I was right.

I quickly checked my reflection in the rearview mirror and ensured my honey-blonde hair was tucked under my hairnet. I wasn't wearing makeup, although I didn't need it. The freckles that had haunted me since childhood had diminished to a gentle dusting over my nose but I had been lucky enough to keep my youthful complexion. I looked tired, though, a slight darkness shadowing my usually bright eyes. It didn't matter—I had no one to impress at work.

No one to impress at home, either, I reminded myself dryly. Also not known for my social life.

Yeah, I wasn't known for a lot of things.

I pulled my keys from the ignition and started toward the side entrance. As I approached, at least fifty dayshift workers were milling about, chattering amongst themselves. Some had cigarettes dangling from between their lips while others were scowling, peering at Waxman Textiles, infuriated.

"What's going on?" I asked one of my coworkers. "Our shift starts in five minutes. Why is everyone out here?"

"We're locked out," Robin grunted.

"What?" It didn't make any sense. Most of us had worked

here for years. If there was some kind of problem, we would have at least gotten an email ... wouldn't we?

On a whim, I pulled out my cell and checked my emails for an update but there nothing was nothing that indicated why we were standing around like fools.

I moved toward the door and pulled on it, feeling silly when it didn't give. Obviously, it had probably been done before.

"What a cowardly, shithead thing to do!" some guy yelled. I think his name was Thomas. He looked like a Tom.

"Don't jump to conclusions," I said, holding up my hand. I could feel tension brewing from a mile away and the last thing I wanted was to be in the middle of a riot, especially without all the facts.

"What else can it be?" Tom shot back. "They ain't giving us a paid vacation!"

Suddenly, the side door opened and, in a swarm, we marched toward Brad, the day manager, a rush of inquiries filling my ears.

"What's going on?"

"Are we working today or not?"

"Is there a setback?"

"What the hell is this?"

In a flash, Brad slapped a piece of paper on the door and ducked back inside.

A weird silence followed his departure and I was left dumbly staring at Robin.

"What does it say?" someone yelled and again, we all swept forward in a wave, craning our necks to read the notice Brad had pasted to the door.

"You have got to be shitting me!" Tom howled. "They're laying us off! Just like that! No notice, nothing!"

An uproar began and I wanted to get out of there before shit started flying.

I backed out from the angry mob of workers, retreated to my car, and observed from there. My heart was hammering in my chest as the gravity of what had happened struck me.

I was unemployed. One minute, I'd had a comfortable job, a guaranteed paycheck and insurance benefits; the next, I was locked out and left for broke without so much as a handshake and "good luck."

Look at them, I thought grimly, watching as the workers began to pound on the entrance. What good will this do?

I couldn't sit around gaping at my workplace all day, but it was like a train wreck and I couldn't look away until my cell rang several minutes later.

"Hon, did you just get locked out of Waxman?" my mother crooned in my voice. She sounded as stressed out as I felt.

"Yeah ... how did you hear about it so fast?"

She sighed heavily. "It's a small town, Leila. Jake Watts called. He's livid. He has four kids to support!"

I closed my eyes and shook my head. We weren't unionized. There was nothing we could do unless we hired a lawyer to clap back and Waxman must have known we had no means to do that.

How can we, when the pay was minimal?

"This day is a write-off," I asserted, and Mom soundly commiserated.

"Come over, sweetie. I'll bake a pie."

I laughed. Her solution to everything was baking or cooking. My mom was a quintessential housewife. That classification was derogatory in our ever-changing society but she'd have said the same thing.

Nothing made her happier than caring for her husband and kids, even though we were all grown and living on our own.

She'd married my dad just out of high school and spent her life caring for the four of us, working not a single day. What was peculiar in today's world came naturally to Mom, like she was from another era. It didn't bother her in the least that other women had full-time careers. In her mind, being at home with her family was the right thing to do.

All she needs is a gaggle of grandkids to spoil and she'll be content.

My sister Cat was a newlywed and my brother, Ryan, had recently married as well. I knew kids were in the near future.

I ignored the stab of envy and refocused on what Mom had suggested. I considered her offer. My day was freed up, after all. What else could I do but go home and stress about being unemployed?

And she baked a delectable pie.

"All right, Mom, I'll be there in fifteen."

Outside, a real riot was breaking out and my jaw clenched as I watched my colleagues hurling random items at the building. A part of me wanted to stop them but the meek side of me won, as always. Conflict was not my thing and conflict resolution was hardly my specialty. What could I possibly say to a bunch of desperate people to make them stand down, anyway?

"Hey, morons, they've got the property damage you're causing on camera!"

"Tom, you can't break into the building with a cinderblock!"

It was better to just opt out of here. I backed out of my space and left the lot, my eyes darting worriedly to the rearview mirror. Security joined the assembly. Thankfully, I was the hell out of there. A criminal record was not on my list of wants; my prospects were bleak enough as it was.

It took me less than fifteen minutes to get to my parents' place. Only after I parked in front of the perfectly manicured lawn did it dawn on me that I had defied all the speed limits, putting as much space between me and the factory as possible.

My heart was still beating fast as I made my way up the flagstone. A light snow had fallen overnight and it dusted the Thanksgiving decorations Mom had put out. A plywood turkey eyed a cornucopia filled with squash and a huge real pumpkin sat on the front porch.

Mom put a lot of effort into her décor but it was hard to feel festive today, not when a cloud of gloom seemed to have befallen Alpena.

I should have stayed in bed this morning, Wrapping the jacket around me, I stepped onto the wraparound veranda. I blamed my lethargy on the cold but maybe I'd sensed the bleakness of the day instinctively.

Too late now—I was facing whatever was in store for me.

Mom must have been watching from the window because the door flew open the second my foot hit the landing. She peered at me with worried blue eyes.

"Oh honey," she said sympathetically, extending her arms to me. "Come here."

Instantly, I threw myself into her arms, relishing the warmth of her bosom. My feelings shone clearly on my face, no matter how hard I tried to hide them.

"It's fine." I didn't separate myself from her embrace. "I'll find another job."

"Of course you will!" Carla Butler conceded firmly. "You have many talents!"

Sometimes I wondered how she managed to lie with such a serious face. The fact was I didn't have many talents. I'd graduated high school, but much to my dad's chagrin, I'd never attended college.

"You're the only one who did not go to college!" he protested. "Why not?"

"Because I don't know what to do with my life and will not waste your money on a degree I might never use."

"Leila, a college education is important! At least a trade school like Morris!"

"I'm not going to be a mechanic like my brother, Dad."

No, I thought with sarcasm, pissed for not listening to my father five years ago. Instead I'll work a menial job and get laid off on a whim. That is a much sounder plan.

Waxman had been the first and only job I'd ever had. It had been supposed to be something to guide me to where I wanted to go, but what direction was that? Even still, I had no idea.

"Come on, sweetie. Help me cut the apples."

We untangled from one another and I followed my mom into the kitchen.

"Whoa! Are you opening a pie shop?" I asked, noting the pile of apples on the kitchen island. "

"I'm making a few pies," she replied defensively. "I'm taking them to the neighbors and ..."

To my astonishment, she bit her lower lip, blinking back some tears. It was not difficult to surmise where my heart-on-the-sleeve responses were from. Mom could cry at the drop of a hat. She could full-on sob at cat-food commercials.

"Mom! What's wrong?" I demanded, rushing to her side. "Why are you crying?"

"Oh," she uttered, waving her hand and blinking rapidly. "It's just so sad. I, I'm making some pies for the Jensens."

My back tensed and I parked on a stool at the counter, nodding slowly.

"I see ..."

Because the entire topic was too painful, I did not insist, but had to know and if anyone had an answer, it was Mom.

"What is happening over there?"

She looked at me in shock, her eyes widening. "You didn't hear about what happened?"

"I did," I replied quickly. "I only meant ... what's happening with Micah now?"

My mom took her own seat, peering at me from across the counter, her mouth pulled into a fine line of regret.

"Well, I imagine he'll go to Children's Services," she sighed. "That's what happens when you lose both your parents ..."

She choked on the last words, making me shudder. I swallowed and shook my head, the now-familiar sorrow filling my heart. Micah was an orphan; his parents dead from a misfortune.

How much worse could it be for a kid of ten?

The only thing worse was the estranged older brother re-entering Micah's life.

Jayce Joyce is too self-centered to return to Alpena. Micah is better off without him ... isn't he?

3

JAYCE

Most of the people at the house were strangers to me, and they certainly didn't know me, but that didn't stop the dirty looks I was getting.

My parents' neighbors and friends filtered through the house, mumbling empty platitudes into my ears, but I didn't hear it. I was still in shock, stunned this had taken place.

"It was a drunken truck driver who hit them, Mr. Jensen. He was on the wrong side of the interstate as your father was driving. He tried to swerve but ... death was instant ... fortunately, Micah was at a sleepover ... make arrangements ..."

What the cop said still flittered in and out of my subconscious. Most of it was baffling, partly because I wasn't there in mind at all. My thoughts wondered why I hadn't made amends with Dad when I'd had the chance to make things right. Why had he always been so damned stubborn?

I didn't even bother to answer the door when someone rang the bell any longer. The kid who I assumed was my brother did that, although I wouldn't have recognized him on the street if I'd seen him. Micah looked nothing like the six-year-old I'd left behind almost four years ago. However, he looked like the young man from my dream.

The premonition stayed, hovering over me like an umbrella, and every time I closed my eyes, trying to block the outside world, it would flood back in a torrent.

The kitchen my mom had loved so much was overflowing with casseroles and roasts, pies and breads. It appeared like a buffet had vomited inside; the smells of the food made me nauseous. I wished people would stop coming in, but in a town the size of Alpena, peace wasn't something easily found. They meant well, but I wished they do it somewhere else.

"Just lock the damned door!" I finally snapped at Micah, my nerves stretched to their breaking point. "No more people!"

He looked at me with blank eyes and the expression slightly chilled me. There was no emotion in his face, nor any sadness or depression. It was like he was elsewhere and his body moved around on autopilot.

"YOU lock the damned door," he snapped back. Even though I'd started it, his attitude jolted me.

Without a word of rebuke, I rose from the chair and approached the front door, hoping to close it before another person came by offering condolences, but of course, I wasn't so lucky.

Two women were coming up to the porch, and for a twisted second, I wanted to slam the door in their faces until it flashed upon me that I actually knew them. Well, I recognized her anyway.

I couldn't remember the last time I'd seen Leila Butler, but certainly, whenever it was, she had not looked like this.

A vague recollection of a freckled-face blonde with wide, pensive eyes and slightly bucked teeth was in my mind.

Braces and corrective surgery had done miracles on the lithe, tall woman in a simple white T-shirt under a long cardigan and pair of form-fitting jeans that left nothing to the imagination. Despite the inappropriateness of the situation, as she neared the door with her mother, I found myself gawking at her.

Carla Butler was holding a stack of pies in her hands and froze when her eyes rested on me.

"Jason!" she gasped. "Y-you're here!"

My brow furrowed at the absurdity of the disclosure.

"Of course I'm here. Where else would I be?"

The Butler women exchanged glances and Carla looked at me again but Leila shifted her eyes away. I got the sense she was still checking me out peripherally, but it was tough to discern. Maybe it was just wishful thinking not to feel like such a pervert for gawking at her.

"I, I'm sorry for your loss, Jason," Carla said, holding out the pies. "I admired your mother a lot. And your father."

She added Dad as an afterthought. He really had been a prick.

And now he was dead.

"Thanks," I grunted, accepting the desserts. I didn't know how much the neighbors supposed we could consume, but most of it would certainly go to waste.

"H-how are you holding up?" she asked. Yet another stupid question, but I kept studying Leila's profile.

"Fine." I wished Leila looked at me but she was distracted by something else.

"Hi, Micah," she called.

My brother joined me in the entrance. "Hi, Leila!"

There was genuine emotion in his voice and his eyes brightened up.

Oh, look at that—he is in there.

Micah pushed past me and stepped onto the porch, looking up at Leila with shining eyes.

"I'm so sorry about your mom and dad," she sighed softly,

stooping down to meet him at eye level. "Is there anything you need? Anything I can do for you?"

As if I wasn't even there! I was beginning to take it slightly personally. After all, I'd lost my parents too. Where was her compassion for me? I hadn't been asked if I needed something.

Or was I being egotistical?

To my annoyance, Micah turned and looked at me, his dark eyes narrowing. Leila also peered at me for the first time with contempt.

What the hell is this? Why is she looking at me like that? I haven't seen her since she was a teen! Anything she heard about me is secondhand. What a judgmental bitch!

Deliberately, Micah turned to her again and shook his head, but the message was clear—he didn't want me there.

"No," he assured. "I'm fine."

Leila straightened up and intentionally avoided eye contact but I could tell she wanted to stare me down. As if I was somehow responsible for everything that had happened.

Have I walked into an ambush?

I recognized the sense of ire growing in my stomach. I felt it every time I returned to Alpena.

Here I am, back again, and facing everyone's scrutiny.

"Do you have a cell?" Leila asked my brother, but her voice was low as if she'd suddenly realized her mom and I had too much interest in the exchange. A red tinge touched her face.

"Of course."

"Get it and I'll program my number in it. Call me anytime you need anything."

I had never seen anyone move as fast as Micah in that instant, leaving me and the Butler women awkwardly gaping at one another.

Carla nervously cleared her throat and shot her daughter an odd look.

"And ... Jason, of course you can call us too," Carla offered lamely, but decidedly, the sentiment did not extend to me.

"Sure," I grunted. "Thanks."

"Have you made arrangements for the ... services?" Carla asked timidly. "We would like to pay our respects."

I nodded. "Friday at four is the funeral. There's a viewing on Thursday from 3-7 p.m. at Chapel Rock."

"We'll be there," Carla assured me. Oddly, I took comfort in knowing that, even though I sensed the near animus oozing from her. It was good to know there would be two familiar faces in the sea of angst and brimstone.

"Great." It was not easy to be grateful when their thoughts were clear—they didn't think I belonged there.

I don't want to be here either! I'm supposed to be in LA, meeting with Sony right now, not accepting desserts and empty sentiments from strangers.

Shit! Sony.

As impossible as it seemed, I'd forgotten about the meeting. My cell had been off since I'd boarded the plane in LA, and I had not bothered to turn it on again when I got to Michigan.

"Excuse me." Micah came running back to the door, but I brushed past him.

He didn't need me—he'd made that much clear from the minute I arrived. He had more friends than me in Alpena.

The flight had been a blur; the cab ride to the house and the conversations with the people did not register in my mind yet. Not a single person cared enough about me, but slowly, the haze was lifting from my eyes and I located my cell in the pocket of my jacket. I needed to touch base with Daryn, at the very least. The rest of the band could wait.

When I turned on the phone, it exploded with texts and voicemail notifications. I barely managed to open my contacts when it rang again. It was Daryn. She probably had been trying incessantly to get through.

"Hey." It was the only word I could muster. She didn't give me time to create a sentence.

"Hey? Fucking HEY? Is that what you're saying to me? Do you realize how much you dropped the ball? I sent a limo to your house at 8:30 this morning. A fucking Hummer, Jayce, fully stocked with a—"

"My parents died last night."

At least I knew what her surprise was. Too bad I couldn't muster the least bit of excitement.

The silence which followed could've been cut with a knife. I fell back on the bed in the guestroom, blankly staring at the ceiling. Out of the blue, the reality hit me like a thousand tons of mass.

"What?" Daryn finally managed to say. "Jayce, are you serious?"

I inhaled deeply but couldn't breathe, not really. My chest hurt and I was almost in tears.

Goddamn it!

I gritted my teeth together, trying to catch my breath.

"Jayce, are you there?"

"Yeah." The word barely managed to get out.

"What happened? Where are you?"

"I'm in Michigan. The funeral's in a couple days."

"Christ, I am so sorry, Jayce. Obviously if I'd known, I wouldn't have gone off on you. Why didn't you call me?"

The answers couldn't formulate—my mind wasn't working that way yet.

"Can you do me a favor?"

"Anything! Do you want me to come down there? Do you need me to make arrangements? Tell me!"

"NO!" The last thing I wanted was for her to come. The next

few days were inconceivable, and Daryn shouldn't see me in pieces. In her presence, things were purely professional, and there was no cause for her to see me unstable, no matter the circumstances.

"No," I said again, with less emotion. "Just tell the guys what's up. Did you go to the meeting today?"

"Never mind the meeting."

The answer filled me with dismay. It was enough—I'd screwed the opportunity; the one we'd been busting our asses for. The guys would never forgive me.

"Will you do that?" I was floating again, somewhere else, somewhere by the ceiling. I barely recognized myself, lying there on the bed. There was no semblance of the brooding rockstar. Suddenly I was a little boy who'd lost his parents, making sense of everything that was happening.

"Of course I will," Daryn sighed. "Are you sure you don't want me to come out there?"

"I'm sure."

"Okay, Jayce …if there's anything you need, anything at all …"

"I'll be in touch. My phone may be off sometimes."

"I won't bother you. Call anytime."

I nodded even though I knew she couldn't see me and disconnected the call without saying goodbye.

Remaining in my spot, looking at the white swirls on the ceiling, trying to make sense of the lot. The more I thought, the less coherent my life seemed.

A knock on the door shifted my attention and even though I didn't answer, it opened anyway.

Carla Butler stood at the threshold, looking uncomfortable.

"Jason …"

I turned my head toward her without sitting up. I thought about telling her my name was Jayce, but it wasn't worth the energy. She didn't care what my name was anyway.

"Leila and I are going to stay for a while, if you don't mind. Micah has asked us."

My body heaved into a vertical position.

"No need for that. We've got this."

"Well ... you have a visitor," Carla announced.

"So? People have been coming in and out all day."

"No, Jason, this is someone different."

Why was she being so enigmatic and not saying what she wanted to say?

"Mrs. Butler, with all due respect, my headspace is not ready to play twenty questions."

"It's your parents' lawyer."

What!? Not that I had experience in these matters before, but it seemed an odd time to be discussing the estate, didn't it? My parents weren't even out of the morgue yet.

"Now?"

Carla looked at me awkwardly and lowered her eyes.

"This needs to be dealt with sooner rather than later, Jason."

Again, I wished she'd speak in layman's terms for my overwrought mind. She seemed to sense my chagrin but when she spoke again, the world turned that much darker.

"Custody of Micah, Jason. Your parents named you his guardian in the event of something like this."

4

LEILA

I wasn't happy about staying at the Jensen's, but what choice did I have, really? Micah wanted us there, and the lawyer had insisted on seeing Jayce. It wasn't good for the boy to be alone, even for a few minutes, not when his grief was so fresh.

Jayce and the attorney were downstairs in the living room while I stayed with Micah in his room. What was Mom up to? She was probably eavesdropping on the meeting, even though she had no business. Naturally, I wasn't going to stop her.

"What'll happen to me now?" Micah asked unexpectedly.

I zoned in. "What do you mean?"

"Am I going to foster care?"

A wave of goose bumps followed his words and before I could stop myself, I quickly shook my head.

"Oh no, Micah, of course not!"

Why had I said that? I had no idea would happen. I couldn't imagine Jayce would stay in Alpena and take care of him—he'd ditched his family years ago—or at least that's what I'd heard.

He'd left for LA in my early teens and the talk around town was that Jayce was a lost rebel who only cared about creating songs. Four years ago, he had been here for Christmas and never looked back.

I'd lie if I said I didn't look for his music on Spotify. He had one of those voices, the kind that sent shivers down your spine when he sang. The man had talent, but talent didn't represent character. Undoubtedly.

Why was he so damned handsome? It made it harder to look at him with wariness when those dark, chocolate eyes bored into my soul. I sensed he was demanding my attention, forcing me to gaze at him, and it drove me crazy—it was almost impossible to resist!

"Isn't it why that man is here? To take me away?" Micah insisted, and again, I was dragged into the present.

"No! Micah, that man is ..."

Was, my brain corrected automatically, but I didn't say it.

"That man is your parents' lawyer. He's here to talk to Jayce about legal issues."

"Like what's going to happen with me."

When did kids get so smart? Did I know what legal issues were at his age?

You didn't lose both your parents at his age, I reminded myself, and my heart swelled with sadness.

"That is the number-one priority," I told him quietly. "But Micah, you have aunts and uncles, don't you?"

"Not in the state."

Maybe he would go live with them out of state? No matter what happened in that meeting, Jayce probably wouldn't take on the care of his little brother ... or would he?

How could I make that judgment? I didn't know the guy, and even though, earlier, I had been determined to hate him, he wasn't making it simple, even with the sullen attitude.

People in pain lash out. I'm sure he's not always a grouch.

"Whatever happens, you'll be with people who love and care for you," I told Micah firmly. "You don't need to worry."

It was the best I could muster.

"If you say so," he grumbled without conviction. Had I made matters worse? What if he did go to foster care? He'd loathe me for lying.

"Knock knock," my mom called from the slightly ajar door. She was bearing a tray of milk and pie.

"Here," she said, lowering the silver serving dish onto Micah's dresser. "I brought you something to eat. Leila, can I have a word with you?"

Micah seemed more fascinated by Mom's apple pie than with what was going on.

I rose from my spot on the floor and followed her into the hallway. We stood at the top of the stairs. Mom's face was wrought with worry.

"Jason is getting custody of Micah," she said, out of Micah's earshot.

It was a predictable response, after all. Although disappointed, I didn't know whether to scoff or shrug. I'd hoped for better for him.

"I'm surprised Beth and Gary named him guardian," I offered. "Considering how they felt about him."

"I'm not."

Mom wanly smiled at me.

"There is no greater bond in the world than that of siblings," she gently explained. "They share the same DNA. Who better to take care of Micah than his own brother? Like it or not, they're an extension of the same people."

Although she had a point, it was hardly the reason to dump a little boy on a stranger who couldn't sit in one place.

"Jayce doesn't know Micah!" I exploded, feeling abnormally angry. "Micah doesn't want to live with some misanthrope!"

"That's what I'm saying," Mom sighed. "Jason is not a stranger, even if they've been estranged. Gary and Beth knew what they were doing."

"You think so?"

My back stiffened as Jayce appeared on the landing, his face crimson with anger. I hadn't even heard him coming up the stairs. Ashamed, Mom and I looked exchanged glances, and then examined the floor.

"You think leaving a ten-year-old kid with me is 'knowing what they're doing'? Because I don't see it that way." His eyes flashed with indignation. "I see it as my father slapping me in the face one last time from the grave."

He thought his own father was sticking it to him, as if providing comfort and stability to Micah was some great punishment.

The only comfort he's worried about is his own. That's why he's so angry.

"This is all quite a shock to you right now, Jason—" Mom started to say, but he scoffed and threw his hands up.

"You don't know a thing about my life, Carla," he barked, turning his back to us. "Just because you heard my parents' side doesn't mean you know the first thing about me. My name, for example. It's Jayce. Jayce Joyce."

He bolted back down the stairs, leaving us staring at one another. A combination of pity and anger filled me.

"You should talk to him," Mom suggested, and I chuckled dubiously.

"Me? Why? I have no recommendations."

I'd likely aggravate him more, if anything. And it might not even upset me.

"You're removed from this, Leila. He won't see you as the enemy. He's hurting right now and he needs someone to talk to.

He's not snapping because he's mad; he's snapping because he's in pain. It's the first stage of grief, dear. Go talk to him."

Why had I become this person? The look in my mom's eyes left little room for argument. The man had just lost his parents and learned he was responsible for a ten-year-old. I should cut him some slack and muster up some compassion, even if I wanted to reserve it all for Micah, who deserved it more.

"Fine."

I found Jayce staring blankly out the kitchen window. He didn't see me at first as I admired his chiseled, scruffy profile.

The gray light of the afternoon was fading into evening, the days getting so much shorter. Thanksgiving was next week, and I wondered if Jayce had anything to be thankful for.

By the look on his face, he didn't seem to feel blessed. His jaw was locked in place and his dark eyes were glowing with intense emotion. Why was my heart doing this?

"Are you going to stand there gaping at me, or did you come down here for a reason?"

A flush of heat touched my face.

"I, I came down to see if you were okay." The words sounded ridiculous as they met my ears. Of course he wasn't okay. Even if he was a selfish prick, he couldn't be "okay" under this state of affairs.

"Leila, I don't need a babysitter."

He remembered my name.

I wanted to kick myself. Who the hell cared if he remembered my name? Why was that relevant?

"Are you going to stay in Alpena?"

I decided to cut to the chase. Beating around the bush was getting me nowhere, and how could I manage small talk with him when he looked so angry, so ... defeated?

"I don't really have a choice right now, do I?" he shot back.

Tentatively, I made my way into the kitchen and paused across the counter.

"You always have a choice," I told him softly. "I understand you have relatives that can be with Micah."

His head jerked, and he glared at me like I was on fire.

"I'm not sending Micah to live with people he doesn't know!"

That was not the expected answer.

"He doesn't know you either, Jayce."

The expression on his face told me it was the wrong thing to say, but it was too late.

"If you came down here to make me feel like shit, you've succeeded," he growled, turning away from me. "I'm not dumping my brother on an uncle who couldn't be bothered to send a Christmas card once in thirty years or an aunt who has sixty cats. But thanks for noting my options."

The sarcasm was thick and laced with fury.

"I came here to see what I can do to help." I realized I was stepping closer to him. I reached out to touch his muscled bicep through the thin red cotton long-sleeve. It flattered his smoldering darkness perfectly.

Jayce turned his head and looked at my hand but didn't move.

Slowly, his eyes moved up along my neck until they rested on my face. I was blushing but didn't know what else to do—yank my hand away? It felt like I was being electrified by the contact. I shouldn't have touched him, but I couldn't walk away, not when I might be reaching him, if only a bit.

Deliberately, his hand slipped over mine, my fingers lost beneath the wide, calloused palm. I was dizzy.

This is wrong on so many levels.

"You know how you can help?" he asked in a gruff and low voice. A shiver slithered down my body as I waited for him to finish.

"Yes," I breathed. "Tell me what to do."

Abruptly, my fingers were being unpeeled from his bicep and he tossed my hand aside with scorn.

"You can mind your own damned business. You and your mother. If you think you can get dirt on what's happening in this house by pretending to give a shit, you've got another thing coming."

With that, he tramped out of the kitchen, leaving me gaping after him in astonishment. Humiliation flooded my face and tears of indignation burned. I gritted my teeth together.

He's an asshole.

"He's in pain." My nosy mom overheard everything. "But don't give up on him."

I snickered mirthlessly. "I think he made his sentiments pretty clear, Mom. He thinks we're just being busybodies. We should leave."

"Leila, do you know what a wounded animal does?"

"Mom, I—"

"It lashes out when someone tries to help and then, when it's certain no one will come for it, it dies alone."

The idea of another death in the Butler family nagged me. Mom was being metaphorical but it still made my skin crawl. If something happened to Jayce, Micah would really be alone.

"Even though it needs help, it will push everything away to die alone. Isn't that something?" Mom concluded. She seemed proud of herself for coming up with that.

"First of all, Jayce is not a wounded animal. Secondly, I wouldn't help a wounded animal if it tried to wound me."

"Sure you would," Mom laughed. "It's in your nature. You're a fixer, darling, just like me. In fact, you're a lot more like me than you suppose."

I wished she wouldn't say stupid shit like that. I didn't like arguments, that was true, but would not put myself at risk to help some unlikable guy—pain or no pain.

I thought of my coworkers rioting at the factory. I might have been able to stop them but hadn't..

And I liked them. I doubt Jayce Joyce is even tolerable.

"I'm going home. Are you coming?"

"You're leaving?" Micah cried. "I thought you would stay for a while."

I forced a smile, ignoring my mom's knowing look. How long had he been standing by the kitchen wall, snooping? I wracked my brain for what we chatted about.

"I can stay for a while longer, Micah." I was doing it to look after him. Someone had to if his brother wouldn't, right?

I caught sight of movement in the dining room but no one was there. Was Jayce listening to us?

Why do you care? You're here for Micah, not him.

But even then, who I was kidding?

5

JAYCE

Daryn showed up for the funeral. I honestly wished she hadn't—her presence made an impossible situation a thousand times worse. I maintained my composure, although I probably would have even if she hadn't materialized. Losing it in front of strangers was not something I envisioned doing, no matter what the stress level was.

My bandmates were still in the dark about what had happened and even Daryn didn't know I would be stuck in Alpena until I figured out how to bring Micah with me to LA.

At least that was the plan. More than likely, reality was going to be much more difficult. Changing schools, dealing with the house—that was just off the top of my head. What would that entail?

Los Angeles was no place to raise a kid, and candidly, how would Micah respond to getting swept away from the only life he'd ever known? Indisputably, he had friends, although I never saw one come by. Maybe he'd told them to stay away. Not like I was here often enough anyway.

Under the best of circumstances, my brother barely spoke to me. He hated me, like everyone else in this town. I had no clue how to converse with him. Not much to explain a kid why I'd left. Until he was old enough and chasing his own rainbows, I guess he wouldn't understand. Or maybe he would be like Father and think I'd been a self-interested fool.

Micah probably would just have holed himself up in his room, playing Mario Cart all day, if it hadn't been for Leila. He went with her on errands and she took him away from the doom and gloom of the house. When she stayed, they played boardgames or video games.

I looked forward to Leila's visits as well. It broke up the monotony as I tried to get my thoughts mended.

So many things to consider! I was a homeowner, and Micah's custodian. I still had a house and career to worry about in LA. And here I was; wasting away, taking no steps to do something productive. Truthfully, I didn't even know where to start.

When she came to the house, Leila avoided me, spending all her time with Micah, but I stole glimpses of her whenever possible. It was still difficult to reconcile that she was the same girl I vaguely remembered from youth.

The way I'd treated her the day after my parents died was shameful, but apologies weren't my forte. The entire thing could be forgotten, but she wouldn't even meet my eyes.

"How are you holding up?" my agent asked after the service. My parents had been laid to rest in Chestnut Field Cemetery, on the outskirts of Alpena. I couldn't believe how many people showed up. My parents had been greatly respected, and a spark of pride touched me learning of everything they'd done for Alpena; stuff I'd had no idea about.

It also made me feel like shit. They had been so appreciated in Alpena. Mom's volunteer work at the hospital; my dad's endless donations to charity …

"I'm all right," I lied to Daryn, making my way back to the hired limo to take Micah and me to the graveyard. He was already in the car and I moved slowly, knowing he was crying. I didn't want to interrupt his grief.

It had finally hit him and he couldn't keep it together. He screamed at me to leave him alone before retreating into the car.

He's so much like Father ... so much like me. He wants no one to see him in pain.

That might not be a good thing, but I was at a loss on how to handle it.

I knew music, not parenting. What to do with a little brother who was determined to hate me?

"I spoke with the band," Daryn remarked as we paused outside the limo. "They send their condolences and want you to call when you're up for it."

"I'm up for it! I just have a lot going on!"

Daryn smiled thinly. "You know what I mean, Jayce. They will not hassle you, but would like to hear from you."

They want to know how long their careers are going to be stalled by this. I didn't bother to voice my understanding. It wasn't Daryn's fault or any of the guys. No one could have foreseen this. Calling them was one more thing to do on my list—but it was near the bottom.

"Thank them for the wreath they sent. I'll call them soon."

Daryn pensively observed me with her wise gray eyes.

"So you're planning on being here for a while?"

"I don't know!" My nerves were far too stretched to make any decisions. "Christ, Daryn, my parents aren't even in the ground yet. Some lawyers want to slap civil suits on the semi driver. I have neighbors offering their unsolicited advice ... A kid to worry about—"

Daryn reached out and clutched my arm. My outburst was boisterous. It had been unintentional.

"I am not pressuring you," she interjected. "I am trying to lend a hand. The meeting with Sony ..."

My heart stopped. I clenched my teeth together, expecting what she would say.

"I know," I sighed. "It was a bust."

She didn't say anything but she didn't have to. All the same, I was grateful she didn't rub it in.

As he saw us approaching, the chauffeur hurried around to open the door but Daryn did not let go of my arm.

"Jayce, we are here for you, all right? I know you like to do things on your own, but you don't have to."

I wasn't listening because Micah wasn't alone in the limo. Leila was inside, cradling my brother in her arms. Micah was asleep, his face streaked with tears. Something welled in my chest as I stared at them; the sweetness of it pierced me.

Leila's blue eyes clouded when she saw Daryn clinging to my arm. Her full lips twitched and she lifted her index finger to her mouth, indicating to be quiet, before returning her hand to caress Micah's dark waves.

"I'll be in touch," Daryn whispered, leaning forward to dart a kiss on my cheek. My eyes were still fixed on Leila as I climbed inside.

The driver softly closed the door, so as not to wake Micah. He didn't stir.

"Your girlfriend?" Leila asked with a note of scorn in her voice.

"My agent."

A look of sheepishness crossed over her face but she didn't look into my eyes.

"He cried himself to sleep," she whispered. "He needed it."

I nodded but couldn't tear my eyes away from her. She was so natural with Micah, so tender. She knew how to handle him.

"The residence, Mr. Jensen?" the driver asked quietly.

I shook my head. "Can you drive around for a while? I don't want to wake my brother."

That was only half of it, really. I really wanted the time with Leila. I was seeing her in a completely different light; maybe she wasn't a nosy neighbor, criticizing me, but someone on my side.

It was a foreign feeling, and not one I easily embraced.

My mom's sister, Helen, and my dad's brother, Fred, were staying at the house so they could greet everyone coming to the reception. No need for Micah and me to hurry back.

"How are you able to visit every day?" I asked. "Don't you work?"

I shouldn't have said it like that. My diplomacy skills sucked.

Leila frowned but shook her head. "I just got laid off from Waxman."

My brow furrowed. I'd heard something about that—the textile plant had locked out hundreds of employees without notice.

Right before the holidays. Classy.

"How long had you worked there?"

"Five years."

Leila Butler did not seem like someone working in a factory. She appeared overly ... exquisite?

"That sucks."

"Yeah." She chuckled.

A minute of awkward silence ensued.

"Any thoughts on what you'll do for work now?"

She eyed me, her fingers lacing through Micah's hair. For a weird second, I got jealous of my baby brother, wishing to lay my head in her lap and let her do the same to me. What would she do if I tried?

Probably slap me.

"I'm searching. It's always tough to find work during the holidays." Her tone confirmed the job market in Alpena was not good.

As the vehicle moved smoothly along the road, my mind was formulating a plan as I gazed at Leila's face. She called me on it.

"Why are you looking at me like that?"

"I'm just thinking,"

"Can you think without scanning me?"

I grinned and sat back in the seat.

"So what about you?" she asked when I didn't speak again. "What are you going to do with your livelihood?"

My grin faded instantly.

"That's a matter for another day," I shrugged.

"Your songs are really good."

I was taken aback.

"You listen to my songs?"

Humiliation colored her face and she shrugged again, turning her head so I wouldn't see the blush on her cheeks.

"I heard a couple."

She was so full of surprises, wasn't she?

"It's been a long road but ..." I trailed off, feeling a pang of regret as I thought about the Sony deal going to hell.

"But what? You're on the radio. I heard you."

I couldn't help but smile.

"There's more to it than getting your music on the air. Although that is a great step in the right direction."

"I don't know much about the music industry," Leila confessed, flushing a deeper shade of red.

"Most people don't unless they're trying to make a name for themselves for many years."

Her head tilted slightly and she peered at me.

"Is it everything you thought it would be?"

I couldn't help but feel she was making a dig at me somehow.

"It's my dream," I answered curtly. "I'm doing what I love, so yeah, it kind of is."

"Do you miss being here?"

How could I explain there was a lot of guilt over what had happened? That I could have been a better son and brother? Like everyone else, she was under the impression I was narcissistic and had left my family without a second thought. It wouldn't matter what I said.

"No."

At least that part was true. Not the small-town gossip and everyone knowing everyone else's business. Although, sometimes, LA could be just as small.

Leila didn't respond to my blunt denial but she appeared put off by it.

So what if she is? I'm not trying to impress her.

Snow started falling again. That was another thing I didn't miss about Michigan—all the damned snow. The gaudy Thanksgiving decorations lining the residential streets seemed much better here, among the falling white flakes, than under the palm trees.

A twinge of nostalgia touched me, and I exhaled deeply.

"Jayce ..."

Leila's bright blue eyes were shining with compassion.

"Yes?"

"I'd be glad to help with Micah if you need it."

That was when it struck me. She needed a job, and my sullen brother needed a companion. Maybe we could work out a deal. I was certainly in a place financially to hire her. Micah liked Leila more than he liked me ...

"Do you want a job?"

A soft expression froze on her face.

"A job?" she echoed. "What kind of job?"

Why was she looking at me like she was wary again?

"Could you help take care of Micah?"

Her shoulders visibly sagged with relief. I wondered what she was thinking.

"I don't need to be paid for that," she giggled. "It's no problem keeping him entertained."

I shook my head. "No, you don't understand. I want you to take care of him full-time when he's not in school. Pick him up and drop him off—do you drive?"

She nodded, but her brow creased.

"Maybe help me out around the house? I might have to go back to LA, so you'd stay with him. Can you cook?"

"I ... yes ..."

"You'd be helping me out a lot, and the kid loves you."

"I ... okay?" She didn't sound convinced.

"What's wrong? I'll pay you whatever you think is fair. It will take a lot of weight from my shoulders, not having to worry about what Micah is up to."

"It's not that ..."

I waited, and she exhaled in a rush, "Are you asking me to move in with you guys?"

Now that I hadn't thought of, but why not? We had the room, and it would probably take the pressure off having Leila as a mediator.

"Yeah, I guess I am. Will that be a problem?"

She shook her shoulder-length blonde mane.

"Not at all. When do I start?"

6

LEILA

Mom was not impressed with my decision but it was too late to back out by the time she knew about it.

"He's got a reputation, Leila! He's ... a ladies' man."

"Trust me, Mom, he's not looking at me as a lover. He's looking at me as a glorified babysitter."

"Make sure it's Micah you're sitting, not Jason."

"Jayce."

"What?"

"His name is Jayce Joyce, not Jason Jensen."

Mom didn't even know how to respond to that but she gaped at me, speechless.

I was on a month-to-month lease for my apartment and gave it up without much thought. It wasn't fancy, and I wasn't overly attached to it, after all. It had just been my first place to call home.

And now I have another place to call home.

The Jensen's house was immaculate. Beth, like my mom, had taken great pride in her dwelling and, between the well-maintained lawns and spotless kitchen, I didn't have a lot of upkeep.

The room that Jayce had given me was twice the size of my apartment, and the bathroom was directly across the hall, although I was sharing it with Micah.

True to his word, the pay was good—honestly more than my wages at the factory. Plus, the style was casual, and no hairnet! What else could I ask for?

The only complaint I had wasn't really a grievance at all; I was growing increasingly attracted to Jayce, the more time we spent together. And we spent a lot of time together.

Even though he claimed he was sorting out his personal affairs, I rarely saw him do more than patter around the house and pick up the guitar. He was still grieving over his parents, even though he obviously didn't want me to know that. In fact, he kept Micah and me at a fair distance, but the three of us always sat down to dinner.

The Thursday I moved in was Thanksgiving, and Mom asked me to come to the house but I declined for the first time ever.

"I'm going to make dinner for Jayce and Micah. They could use some balance around here."

"Well, they can come too!" Mom protested, but I turned it down. It was exciting to make a turkey and all the fixings for the first time. I'd watched Mom do it enough times over the years; certainly, I could handle it.

The football game was playing in the living room and for once, both the men were there together. Every once in a while, I'd hear them yell at the TV and it made me smile.

At first, when Jayce had suggested I move here, I'd thought, like my mom, that he had other things on his mind.

I was a virgin and had no interest in losing myself to a scandalous rock star on a one-night stand.

To his credit, Jayce was never inappropriate. He never leered at me or made me uncomfortable like some men. Maybe all the stories I'd heard about him before he left Alpena had been embellished.

To me, he was a brooding man. But he wasn't a pig, even when he looked at me wistfully from time to time.

No way that'll happen. I peered into the oven. Hours more for the bird, but everything was exactly on schedule.

"Leila, Fergus is here. Can I go out on my bike?" Micah yelled to me. So much for the idyllic moment between the brothers.

"Are you sure, Micah?" I asked, wiping my hands on my apron. I shot Jayce a nervous look, but he didn't meet my eyes. He seemed upset that Micah was ready to do something else. He already was slipping his shoes on at the door.

"You could ask me," Jayce snarled, but Micah ignored him, his dark eyes fixed on me.

"Please, Leila? Dinner's not ready for a while, right?"

I looked out the window and saw the sun poking through the clouds, melting the existing snow in the neighborhood.

"Be careful and be back soon." He anticipated my response, barreling out the door after his gangly friend who waited on the steps.

Jayce gave me a sideways glance as I stood there helplessly, feeling like I'd enabled the ruination of Thanksgiving.

"D-do you want a beer or something?" I offered weakly. He shrugged and I took it as a "yes." When I returned from the kitchen, he looked at me fully.

"Where's yours?"

I laughed shortly.

"Oh, I don't drink," I replied. "But you go ahead."

A half smile formed on his lips and it gave me a slight feeling of apprehension.

"You don't drink, you don't yell, you don't cuss. You're kind of a goody-two shoes, aren't you?"

My shoulders rose inadvertently. He was mocking me.

"You say it like it's a bad thing. I think I'm a good person."

He scoffed and took a swig of his beer. "Will you sit or just stand there staring at me with those judgmental eyes?"

What was he talking about? If anything, I felt bad for him. I wasn't looking at him like that.

He has a heavy chip on his shoulder.

I perched on the edge of the couch and pretended to watch the flat screen. I didn't know much about football.

"He'll despise me forever."

My head jerked toward the opposite end of the sofa where he was sitting.

"He doesn't hate you. He's overwhelmed, Jayce. It'll take time for him to get over this."

"I'd hate me too," he continued. "I would have come back to visit, but my dad ..."

He sighed so heavily, it made my heart break.

"I don't know why people can't let one another live their lives, you know?"

"Parents think they know what's best for us. That's why I moved out—my dad wouldn't get off my back about college."

He glanced at me. "You defied your parents? I'm shocked!"

He was sarcastic, but the tone was almost admiring.

"I didn't know what to do with my life, and I wasn't going to throw money away on college if I had no idea."

"Seems fair. Charlie didn't take it so well?"

"I'm the only one in the family that didn't go to college—well, except for Mom. At least you knew your passion. I still have no idea."

Jayce took another big sip of beer, almost downing half of it.

"You'll find your thing," he said after he it went down. "You're young."

Twenty-three didn't seem so young to me, not when Mom

had already been married by my age, with two kids.

I inched toward him and he didn't seem to notice. What was I doing?

I bit my lower lip and willed him to look at me, but his eyes were set on the game. He had to know I was staring at him. Even though he was being smart by ignoring me, I felt slightly rejected. I sank against the back cushions on the suede sofa and we sat in silence for a long minute.

I guess this is good. There's no attraction on his part, so there's no danger—

I was pinned back into the plush fabric then, suddenly, Jayce's face was inches from mine.

"W-what are you doing?" I choked in shock. My heart was racing, not from fear but excitement.

"What are you doing?" he shot back, not moving. His coffee-colored eyes were glowing. What was he thinking? Did he want to kiss me? Startle me? Was he just looking for a reaction?

Instead of answering, I moved my head forward to brush my lips against his.

All of a sudden the tables turned and he looked at me, astounded, but didn't pull himself away. Our gazes were locked. I felt the tip of his tongue prodding my lips apart. Instantly, I pressed my mouth around him.

His eyes grew wider—he hadn't been expecting such a move. The friction of our tongues clashing inspired him to pounce, pinning me down against the sofa.

What was I doing? I couldn't make out with my boss, the man with whom I'd just moved in! But my reservations were out the window, washed away by a wave of heat surging through my body.

My fingers found the strands of his thick mane of hair and, strangely, I felt him relax, like my hands had a calming effect. His kiss grew gentler, although just as hot.

I was shaking, not violently, but enough. I couldn't control it, like when a chill hits you and seeps directly into your bones. Except this was scorching, and I had no desire to make them—or Jayce—stop.

Goose bumps covered me, and every line of his hard body was against mine, our forms fitting together as if we were a part of the same body but in two beings.

The stubble of his face against my skin escalated the sensation of desire, overriding my common sense as his mouth worked over the curve of my neck.

My logical side wanted to tell him to stop but I wouldn't—couldn't. I'd started it. It was up to him to show some restraint, but I wished him not to.

My nipples became hard, taut, and ready for his tongue. I didn't realize my shirt was off, let alone my bra, but, unexpectedly, I was captive to the suction of his lips.

His strong hands clutched at me, drawing us closer, and my legs moved up along his hips to bring him nearer.

This is so wrong! Some weak voice yelled at me. On every level! You can't do this!

But what came out of my mouth were slow, deep moans filling the living room, over the sound of the football game which still played in the background.

"You taste as sweet as you look," Jayce whispered, almost angrily, as if the realization disgusted him. His face dropped on my flat stomach, fingers curling around the waist of my jeans to yank them off.

I tensed, trying to rise. I wasn't ready for what was coming. I'd never gone this far with someone, this fast.

On my elbows, I stared at him, my heart racing, but I didn't tell him to stop. Jayce sensed my reservations and paused, jeans at my knees, my panties halfway down my thighs.

"Are you okay?" His face was gleaming

I couldn't easily answer that question, so the best I could manage was a nodIt was all he needed. His mouth found the cleft between my legs and with a long, pointed lap, he delved into my core.

It was like he'd been there before and my body jerked upward, almost in astonishment. My legs were locked in place—he didn't even bother to fully remove my pants.

"Oh my!" I whimpered. His hand cupped around my naked ass and I fell back onto to couch, my hand clutching the soft cushions, seeking an anchor in the pleasure driving me up over my own head.

Harder, his tongue moved, the strokes even but fast, his mouth closing around the nub of my center, and when his finger slid inside my soaked middle, I couldn't take any more.

I cried out, feeling the gush spray from between my legs, and he sighed, lapping at me like a hungry dog. My body quivered. I needed him in me. How was this happening? I'd never lost complete control to anyone before, and yet I wanted this guy, this bad boy whom I barely knew, to fully possess me.

Another swell rose in the pit of my abdomen and I realized I was going to cum again.

Twice! In a row! That had never happened to me in my life.

But I didn't fight it and I succumbed fully to him, my nails almost breaking as my hands gripped the sofa. There might be holes in the fabric.

My pants dropped to the floor and my legs became a vise against him.

He moved up my body, his weight crushing into me, his shaft pressing against me, sliding up and down. I was so sensitive, I jumped at the movement; my nerves were so tight they could have snapped.

Our mouths met once more, my ankles locking over his naked buttocks. For a second time, I was the instigator, guiding him inside me without a thought. I tried to cry out, the walls of my center closing around him. He was huge, throbbing, and ready for me, but was I ready for him?

I tensed, alarmed that Jayce could hurt me, but my fears were unfounded. I was far too wet to resist, and my need to have him outweighed the pain.

He filled me, taking my breath away, our mouths still interlocking. His solid body fell into a deep, penetrating rhythm which I easily met, my slender frame bucking upward to meet him until I no longer jumped to his thrusts.

We were locked together, lips, groins, hands; our passion reaching new heights.

Jayce whispered to me, his words jumbled, but the tone of his mellifluous voice bringing me further into the trance-like position.

I was in ecstasy, spilling over him as I came again and again, my pussy locking his cock in me.

He grunted and grew bigger, causing me to gasp, but when his sac slapped against me, tight and ready, I knew he was at the point of no return.

Streams filled me, almost burning me as he exploded. Jayce buried his face in my neck, sending yet another round of shivers through my body. I was close to losing myself in the sensory overload.

He spurted into me for what felt like hours and slowly, the exhilarating, warm feeling I had given into began to fade.

Understanding of what I had done hit me like a slap in the face and I struggled to come to terms with it.

I had just given myself to Jayce Joyce, a man I wasn't even sure liked me, let alone worthy of my virginity.

And now I had to see him every day.

7
JAYCE

Was it a bad idea to sleep with Leila? Of course. Did I regret it? Not for a second.

Maybe she had been tantalizing me from the moment I saw her climbing the walkway with her mother. Perhaps it was seeing how she was with Micah which overrode my nagging conscience and said I needed to have her.

She wouldn't look at me as she laid out the meal she'd labored over. It left me feeling like I'd done something wrong.

"Are you guys fighting?" Micah asked when we sat at the table. The turkey looked mouthwatering, and I was starving.

"No!" we answered in unison, but Leila still wouldn't look at me.

Why is she getting weird over this? It was only sex.

I was lying to myself. What had happened between us had been more than an act of passion. It had been born from a need we both had, a desire to be a part of someone else. Why was she making me feel like I'd violated her?

It pissed me off.

"It seems like you guys are fighting," Micah sighed, reaching for the potatoes. "Are you going to cut the turkey?"

I rose to take the carving knife from Leila's hands and she looked at me, bewildered.

"I know how to carve a turkey, Leila. Sit down and eat."

She didn't argue. At least she looked at me again. We'd barely managed to get our clothes on before Micah returned. I could still smell the scent of sex in the air, intermingled with the succulent aroma of the bird and veggies.

"You sure can cook, Leila," Micah professed, taking a bite of gravy-soaked bread. "I hope you never leave."

The words hung in the air like stale cigarette smoke and I felt guilty. Why was there always so much damned guilt?

"How are the yams?" Leila asked, apparently as uncomfortable as I. Micah couldn't fathom what his words meant to us, obviously.

"This is excellent, Leila," I offered, giving her a warm smile. "I had no idea you were such a Martha Stewart."

She blushed and shyly looked away. Strangely, my heart skipped a beat at the bashful expression on her face.

"It's my first time," she explained, and her face turned even more crimson. She began to sputter.

"I, I mean t-this is my first time cooking a turkey!" she choked, and again, her eyes peeled away from mine.

I was confused. What else could she have meant?

"I'm ready to eat turkey sandwiches for the next month," Micah declared as I continued to work at the bird. My brother was smiling for the first time in a week.

Bringing Leila here was the smartest move I made. She's good for Micah.

She was good for me too. I feel less embittered in Leila's presence; her good nature emanated infectiously through me. Sure, I still clung to the hurt and shame I carried, but was it as bad as when I'd first come back? I didn't think so.

I finished cutting and dove into my plate eagerly. Micah

wasn't kidding. It was decadent, and for a minute, I had to stop. The memory of Mom hit me so strongly, a sob filled my throat.

"Jayce?"

I was on my feet, bolting from the table before the tear became obvious.

What the hell was wrong with me? I'd just had sex; I was sitting down to an amazing meal with a beautiful woman; and my brother was, in fact, smiling. And here I was, ruining everything with an emotional breakdown.

I fell against the door of the master suite, my parents' suite, and broke down, the memory overwhelming me. I had been suppressing all my feelings for so long, they'd come to a head.

"Jayce?"

Leila was knocking on the door. I wanted to tell her to go away. Instead, I let her inside and she saw me, blubbering like a kid.

She didn't say a word but opened her arms and I fell into them, choking my tears.

"I was such a shitty son," I uttered, finally catching my breath. "I always thought I would show them, you know? When I made it big. I'd buy them a house and say I told them so."

"They were proud of you," she told me. I chuckled and remained in her arms. The tears were subsiding.

"They did their best for me, and I slapped them in the face by leaving."

"You didn't leave them, Jayce; you followed your dream. There's a difference. It's not like you abandoned them in their time of need. You had every right to pursue your dream."

I studied her face, hastily wiping the tears from my cheeks.

"Do you really believe that? Because no one else around here does."

She returned my gaze and smiled softly. "I'm not everyone else around here."

No, she wasn't. She wasn't like anyone else around anywhere.

"Things have changed," she continued, and we fell apart, but I kept my eyes trained on her as she spoke. "And you're here now, when it counts. You're here for your brother."

Her words were meant to make me feel better, but they didn't. They were ominous because they were true.

I was here, but for how long? My long-term plan was not to stay in Alpena.

Leila didn't know that, and I wasn't about to tell her, not right now, anyway.

We'd had sex one time—that didn't mean we were in a committed relationship. She was still just here to help Micah, right? Right?

Yeah, I could lie to myself any way I wanted. I had strong feelings for Leila. The longer we lived under the same roof, the worse things were going to become when it was time to say goodbye.

Unless you take her with you to LA.

Wow. I really was getting ahead of myself.

"Come on," I said crustily, turning my head like I was worried she might see what I was thinking by looking at my face. "I ruined your awesome dinner."

"Are you sure you don't need a few more minutes?"

"No," I insisted, opening the door. "Micah is finally some semblance of cheerful and I won't screw that up any more than I already have."

I didn't wait for her to reply before stalking down the hall and down the stairs.

I couldn't think too far ahead, not right now. Things would play out the way they were meant to—just like always. I had to have faith in that.

∼

Micah didn't mention my abrupt departure and we finished our dinner without further incident. Leila had made an incredible pumpkin pie and I ate half of it, fighting with Micah over the last piece.

"I made another one," she laughed. "There's plenty for everyone, boys."

After supper, I helped Leila with the dishes even though she tried to get me to relax.

"If I sit on the couch, I'm going to fall asleep," I warned her. "Let me help you with this. It's the least I can do for the meal you made for us."

"It was my pleasure."

She meant it, and again, I was struck at how ... I dunno, old school she was. I lived in a world where women cared about their looks and what guy drove the nicest car. Leila didn't even care that I was on the brink of signing with Sony. She rarely brought up my life in LA.

I don't remember what we chatted about as I loaded the dishwasher and she scrubbed the pots by hand, but I recall how comfortable it was, like we'd done these domestic chores a thousand times before.

It was hard to image I would ever be at ease in such a situation, but somehow, I was ... until my cell rang.

"Hello?"

"Dude, really?"

I tensed, wiping my hands on a tea towel and turning away from Leila's curious look.

"Hey, Johnny. I've been meaning to call you, man. Things have been hectic around here."

"Yeah, I know." The band's bassist paused and inhaled. "I'm really sorry about your folks."

"Thanks. I got the wreath. I asked Daryn to thank you guys."

"Yeah, she did," Johnny replied quickly. "I get that you're

overwhelmed over there. I hear you've got custody of your brother too."

"Yeah ..."

Johnny paused, and I could tell something was on his mind.

"Well, uh, hey, happy Thanksgiving." I supplied, hoping to move the conversation along. I eyed Leila, who was still busy, but she was listening. Not like I was quiet anyway, and if I wanted privacy, I could have gone elsewhere. Truthfully, I wanted to get back to the idyllic, almost Leave it to Beaver moment I had been sharing with Leila.

"Happy Thanksgiving. We want to work on some stuff without you," Johnny blurted out."

"What does that mean?" I asked, dumbfounded by his statement. "What stuff?"

"We're thinking about going on our own—without you, Jayce."

I felt a weird tingling in my limbs and I stood silent for a dead minute.

"It's nothing personal, man," Johnny continued. That was a lie. It was very personal. They were pissed I'd lost the Sony deal.

And I was livid that they were upset. Like I'd had control over the matter.

"Jayce, say something."

"How long have you guys been planning a coup?" I rasped, finally finding my voice. "Is this your way of kicking me when I'm down?"

"It's not like that," Johnny protested. "We just feel like, given your situation, well, you don't really know what's going to happen, and—"

"Why don't you fucking let me tell you how I'm going to handle my life instead of the other way around?" I roared. Leila dropped a plate, taken aback by my outburst, but I was far too incensed.

"Jayce ... that's the other thing ..." he sighed. "Your temper is out of control, man. You're impossible to work with sometimes."

"I'm imposs—are you fucking kidding me right now? We would have never had that damn contract, all those gigs, fuck, even Daryn, because of me! I'm the goddamned glue that holds everything together!"

"I knew you'd act like this. I shouldn't have called, but I felt like you deserved a heads-up."

"Wow. Thanks."

I disconnected the call before he could say anything else. I didn't want to hear another word out of his mouth.

"Jayce, what's wrong?"

Concerned, Leila was at my side and I was shaking with indignation.

How dare they? After all the blood and sweat! They were waiting for an opportunity to drop me!

"I've just been dumped from the band," I said with a short, mirthless laugh. I whipped the phone against the floor and it shattered into pieces. Leila gasped and stepped back.

When I saw the mild apprehension in her eyes, I was contrite.

"Sorry," I said earnestly, reaching out for her hands. "I shouldn't have done that."

A slow expression of relief crossed over her face and she let me grab her cool palms.

"Why? What did they say?"

"They're mad I lost the Sony deal." That was a true enough answer.

"What are you going to do now?" she asked, and I heard a note of hope in her voice as she stared at me with those wide, guileless eyes.

Maybe it was all a sign from the universe. My parents had died right before I got my biggest break. My band was deserting me. And Leila was standing right here in front of me, practically begging me to say the words.

What could I do with a ten-year-old kid in LA anyway? It wasn't fair to upset Micah more, to take him away from his home and friends.

"Jayce? What will you do?" she pressed. I chewed on the inside of my cheek, not wanting to say the words. If I spoke them, they'd be real.

I forced a smile onto my face and shrugged my shoulders nonchalantly.

"It looks like I'm not going back to LA," I replied. The expression of her beautiful face told me I'd told her precisely what she wanted to hear, but my instincts said I'd made the wrong decision.

I wanted Leila, but I also wanted my dream.

8

LEILA

I was deluding myself, but it was such a good fantasy. I had a perfect life, a man who adored me, and a little boy who admired me. It was too good to be true! I forced myself to ignore the faraway look in Jayce's eyes when he thought I wasn't watching.

He missed his old life, no matter how comfortable I tried to make things.

The Thanksgiving decorations went down and I was pulling the Christmas ornaments out of the basement one afternoon when Jayce startled me.

"I'm just going out to get a tree for us," he told me, twirling the keys to his dad's Mercedes in his hand. "Need anything while Micah and I are out?"

I lowered the box, brushing a strand of hair out of my face.

"How about a kiss?" I asked tentatively. It was weird that I was still ill at ease when asking for affection. We slept in the same bed every night, even though we separated in the morning so as not to confuse Micah. The boy had figured out what was going on between us but it gave Jayce some peace of mind, so I obliged.

This time next year, it will all be perfectly natural. A tiny, snide voice warned me not to get too comfortable.

"That I can do," Jayce chuckled, closing the distance between us. He wrapped me in his arms and gently placed a kiss on my waiting lips. Whether it was the slight distance I felt or the dimness of the basement, I suddenly danced him backward until he hit one of the support beams.

My lips fell over the curve of his chin and my hands fumbled at the buckle of his belt as I moved urgently, overcome by a need to taste him the way he had me so many times before.

"Whoa! What are you doing?" Jayce gasped when I dropped to my knees. I wrested the denim from his sculpted ass, pulling a pair of silk boxers down along with the jeans.

"Leila, oh my—"

He choked on the words as I inhaled him, my mouth fully suctioning around his shaft. I almost gagged. The tip of him filled my throat but that didn't stop me from finishing what I had begun.

Jayce groaned, his whole weight falling against the wood, and my hand snaked up to cup his heavy sac. Massaging him with warm fingers, I fell into a deep, fast rhythm, feeling his shaft tighten with my licks.

"Wow, Leila!"

It only inspired me to work harder, squeezing the base. I was challenging him to explode, and when his fingers found their way into my hair, I knew he wasn't going to resist me.

But just as quickly, he picked me up by my hair, pushing me toward the beam which had just supported his back.

"Oh no," he growled in my ear, his body pressed up against me from behind. "You don't get to have all the fun."

I squealed when he lifted my skirt, slapping my ass hard enough to leave a mark, but that pain was short-lived when his fingers slipped inside me, prodding at my already drenched core.

And then he was inside me, his fingers traveling up to explore my other opening, his huge cock jabbing into me as I bent over to grab the beam.

"God, you're so tight," he choked, but I was crying out as he entered me in two separate ways.

It felt so good and so wrong. I pushed outward against him, wanting him as deep as he could go. Jayce's arm wrapped around my waist for leverage, his thrusts growing so intense, my breath was knocked out of me. I couldn't stand anymore!

I climaxed, feeling my release sliding down the heat of my inner thighs, but I couldn't stop. Over and over, I came, feeling the sensation of all his prods until he, too, exploded.

Jayce moaned, shuddering roughly as his grip around my waist firmed, and I realized I was holding him up as much as he was holding me.

I clenched myself around him as if to expel every drop from his quivering cock until we were both finally spent.

Very slowly, he pulled out of me, and more combined juices gushed down my legs.

I turned around and pouted as he released me.

"Why didn't you let me finish?" It was such a weird thing for me to say. I wasn't that kind of girl—or at least I never had been until this moment. Jayce's expression told me he felt the same way. He scowled slightly.

"What was that about?"

I blushed furiously and tried to smile but it came out more like a grimace.

"I'm just trying to please you like you always please me."

His face softened as he reached to pull up his pants.

"Leila, you do everything for us," he told me. "Sex is about mutual gratification. It's never one-sided."

I was embarrassed, but Jayce cupped my face.

"What's going on, Leila?"

I shook my head and managed a sheepish smile.

"Nothing. All the Christmas cheer is getting to me," I chuckled, but that wasn't it.

"Well, let me see if I can help with that. I'll be back with a tree shortly."

He kissed my forehead and let me go, bounding up the stairs two at a time.

I didn't move.

I was too busy overanalyzing what had happened. The finale was always the same—I was terrified of losing him.

LATER THAT SAME DAY, a letter came. It was from a law firm and addressed to Jason Jensen.

A sinking feeling in the pit of my stomach was growing and it only got worse when Jayce got home and opened it.

His jaw tightened and he shot Micah a look from his seat at the kitchen island. Micah was enchanted with whatever he was watching on TV.

"What is it?" Did I want to hear the answer?

He grunted and shoved the letter at me. Yeah, I didn't really want to know.

I shakily inhaled, a torrent of bad feelings overcoming me. I didn't know Jayce had sought out a lawyer to sue the driver who'd killed his parents.

"Are you doing this?" I placed the offensive letter on the counter.

Jayce's gaze was locked on his little brother.

"You're thinking about it."

Now that I knew him well, his eyes were easy to read.

"Micah will be set for life if we win."

"The man is already facing twenty years in jail for manslaughter, Jayce. Taking him and his family for all he's worth won't bring your parents back."

His eyes narrowed and he looked at me angrily.

"You think I don't know that? It's about the long-term here, Leila. The insurance money will take us so far. In case you forgot, I'm unemployed. I'm not making much sitting around Alpena, not working gigs …"

He probably wanted to add something like "wasting my life" but he stopped himself. The pang in my chest was making it difficult to breathe but I held my ground.

"There are other ways to earn money than to sue an already tortured man." I'd felt so bad for that driver after I'd learned of Beth and Gary's deaths, and my sentiments hadn't changed. His name was Carl Hinkman. He couldn't even afford the bail to await the trial at home. He was already rotting in jail. What was Jayce hoping to accomplish by pursuing this?

It was hard to believe money was his only motivator.

"That's easy for you to say, isn't it?" he shot back, his biting tone stunning me. "You make more money than me right now, and I'm paying you."

My jaw locked in place.

"I can pay my way around here." There was not much conviction in my voice.

"You're missing the point," he snapped, rising from the counter. "What's going to happen now that I'm stuck here in Alpena?"

There it was, out on the table.

He was stuck in Alpena. Whatever we were doing was not good enough for him.

Before I could even think of an appropriate response to what he'd said, Jayce was gone, leaving me with a hammering heart in my chest.

"Dad always said my temper reminded him of Jason."

Micah slipped into the kitchen. I blinked away the tears that had pooled in my eyes and weakly smiled at him.

"I never noticed you have a temper. Want a sandwich? I was just about to make one."

He nodded. The kid was always hungry a lot.

I busied myself at the fridge, willing myself to remain collected.

"Isn't it weird that you're Jay's girlfriend but he pays you to cook and clean?"

I shot him a wary look. So much for keeping Micah in the dark.

"Who says I'm his girlfriend?"

"You sleep together every night, and I'm guessing you have sex."

Aghast, I whirled and stared at him, open-mouthed. What could he possibly know about sex at his age?

I shifted my attention back to the sandwiches.

"Our relationship is ... complicated."

"I can tell. It's nothing like how Mom and Dad were."

That made me sad. I hoped to give Micah some impression of normalcy in the wake of his parents' passing, but Jayce didn't make it easy.

"Every relationship is different," I told him gently.

"Are you guys in love?"

I was not ready for this conversation with anyone, let alone a ten year old.

"Here's your sandwich."

I sat across from him and studied his face.

He looks so much like Jayce. I wonder if he's going to send all the ladies into a tailspin the same way his brother does.

"Well?" he demanded after taking a bite. "Are you?"

"Am I what?" I asked innocently, taking my own bite as I was trying to think of an answer that would satisfy him.

"In love. Are you guys in love?"

"That is a mature topic that should only be discussed between adults."

He snorted at the copout but, to my relief, didn't push the issue. I was supremely grateful he didn't because I didn't know how to tell him that yes, I was desperately in love with Jayce, but possibly the sentiment was unrequited.

9
JAYCE

Our little tiff about the lawsuit blew over, but I couldn't get Leila's words out of my head.

So what if Carl Hinkman was in his own personal hell? He deserved that and so much more for what he did. Jailtime was not enough for taking our parents from us, no matter how Leila felt.

At the same time, any settlement that would impact his family bothered me deeply. It wasn't his wife's fault that he was a piece of shit who had gotten behind the wheel drunk. It wasn't his unborn grandkids' fault that he was a careless bastard. A murderer.

In the end, I dropped the suit quietly, much to my lawyer's chagrin.

I didn't tell Leila, almost like she'd say "told you so" even though she wouldn't. A part of me always waited for the other shoe to drop, like it had with Teresa, sleeping with Miguel.

But Leila wasn't Teresa. She wouldn't rub anything in my face. So why was it so difficult to let her in?

That was going through my head as I shopped for her Christmas present. The obnoxious sound of bells accented the carols piping through the mall's speakers. Everywhere I looked, I saw reminders that the big day was only three days away.

Finding a present for Leila was more difficult than I supposed. Heck, even Daryn had been a piece of cake. I'd gotten her a gift certificate to a spa. It was sort of a peace offering for what had happened with Sony. I hadn't spoken to her for a while. Time had given me a perspective on the matter. I couldn't really fault the guys for wanting to branch out when my own plans were so uncertain.

I assumed Daryn was on board with them, but in my pit of depression, I'd never followed up on it. Without the band, the brand we'd worked so hard to market was nothing with me alone.

Or maybe that's what I kept telling myself? It was easier than thinking about starting over at the bottom and clawing my way up again. I wasn't twenty-one anymore.

The thought of what could have been was pushed aside as I stopped in front of a jewelry store to look at the display.

Buying jewelry was tricky. I wanted to get Leila something to show how much I appreciated everything she had done for us, but did I want her to think I was somehow solidifying our future together?

And why the hell not? Why not have a future with Leila?

The only reason I could think was that we were polar opposites. She deserved a man who was as good and wholesome like her, not a washed-out singer who couldn't keep his band together.

My cell rang, shattering my self-deprecation. I grabbed it from the carrier on my waist.

It was Daryn.

"Merry ho-ho!" she chirped in my ear. "How's daddy-hood?"

"I wasn't expecting to hear from you. I guess you got my gift?"

"I did, and it's funny it came today because I was going to call you anyway."

"Great minds, right? How are things in Tinseltown?"

"I'm up to five Xanax and seven Ritalin a day, so basically, normal. Are you coming home?"

I snorted, thinking she was joking.

"So, are you representing the guys now? Did they find another vocalist?"

"You're kidding, right?" Daryn scoffed. "When those idiots told me their plan, I laughed them right out of my office. You are and have always been the heart and soul of Rune. There is no band without you, and I told them as much."

My heart swelled at her words, but I kept my voice neutral. She was an agent—lying was second nature to her. If what she was saying was true, why hadn't she called me? Maybe she'd tried representing Rune without me and it hadn't gone well.

"Well, it's nice to know you have my back."

"Honey, I've been working my ass off to get everything in order for the last month. That's why I've been off the radar, although I thought you'd given up on the life until I got your gift."

"Get what in order?"

I ventured away from the window and moved toward a bench, flopping onto it as Daryn continued trilling in my ear.

"Sony, of course. Your meeting with Sony."

"I screwed everything with Sony."

Daryn barked out a laugh that reminded me of a Chihuahua.

"You're kidding right? You thought it was over because you didn't show to the meeting?"

"Uh, yeah," I replied slowly. "When you stand up a huge corporation, they usually don't give you another chance."

Daryn howled.

"Oh honey!" she chortled. "Either you've been watching too

many movies or you really don't know the industry. Sony gets stood up sixty times a day. That's what happens when you're working with artists. But they are in the business of making money, Jayce."

"We're having another meeting?" I bolted upright, my mouth gaping.

"You thought they wouldn't? It was just a matter of when. I have you scheduled in the day after the New Year's. Can you make it back January 2nd?"

I was speechless.

"Jayce? Are you still there? God, I hate Samsung! Jayce? JAYCE?"

"I'm here, I'm here!" I uttered before she busted my eardrum. "Yeah, I'll go back. What about the rest of the band?"

"Screw 'em. They want you, Jayce. Those fools made a big mistake dropping you. It's your voice, your sex appeal that sells it. Do you want to call them, or should I?"

Again, I didn't know what to say.

"Fine," Daryn sighed. "You can tell them. Do it on Skype and record it so I can see their stupid faces, all right?"

"Okay."

"I gotta go, babe. Chandra Dillion is here, giving me stink because she thinks she owns my ass."

"All right."

The call dropped and I stared at the cell in my hands, shaking my head.

I wasn't dead in the water—I still had a meeting with Sony!

All the excitement was greatly diminished by the thought of telling Leila and Micah.

Because if this panned out, undoubtedly, I'd go back to LA ... indefinitely.

~

CHRISTMAS MORNING FOUND the three of us downstairs around the brightly-lit tree in our pajamas, drinking hot chocolate and snapping pictures. It was a difficult day for my brother, but he didn't display his emotions; he was so much like me. Like our dad.

Leila gave me a thick, dark red velour robe, a color she liked me in. She never said it but her eyes lit up every time I wore cherry or burgundy.

Micah gave me a watch. It wasn't expensive but he had it engraved with my initials. We weren't snuggling yet, or wrestling, but we were making progress. He certainly didn't seem to hate me as much as he had when I first came back home.

Was I setting everything back by accepting this meeting?

Micah seemed happy with his gifts—a bike and some video games. I saved Leila's gift for last.

When she opened it, her face tinged pink and her head whipped up.

"Oh my God, Jayce!" she choked. "This must have cost you a fortune."

It was worth it, just to see her eyes sparkling against the diamonds as she held them up to her flushed neck.

"May I?" She scooted closer, sliding between my legs as I clasped the necklace around her neck.

"Fancy. Now you'll have to take her out somewhere, for once," Micah cracked.

"Mind your business," I snapped but I realized he was right. We hadn't even been on a real date yet. Any time we went out, Micah was always in tow.

We'll have many dates in LA. Much better places to go there than here.

That was my cue. I cleared my throat as Leila sat back, trailing over her present in awe.

"I got some news a few days ago. Good news."

They both looked at me expectantly. I shouldn't have said anything at all, but how much longer could I put it off? I was scheduled back in LA in a week and from there, things would move very quickly.

My house there was vacant, although a neighbor checked on things. It would comfortably house the three of us. But what about this house? Selling it was a painful idea—our parents had loved this house. They'd bequeathed it to me, hoping I would leave it for Micah.

"Well? Don't keep us in suspense," Leila implored me. "What's your news?"

"I spoke to Daryn and—"

"Who's Daryn?" Micah interrupted. I realized neither of them knew my agent. She'd been at the funeral, but I hadn't introduced them.

"She's my agent in LA."

The light faded from both of their faces in unison.

"Oh."

I wasn't sure which one said it, but the sentiment extended to both of them.

"And," I rushed on before I lost my nerve, "it turns out I still have a meeting with Sony. I need to be back in LA on the second."

"Meeting for what?" Micah asked. Leila turned her head away.

"I have a record deal lined up. The meeting was supposed to happen already but …"

I stopped speaking, not wanting to bring up my parents.

"So what does this mean?" Micah demanded. He could already tell what it meant.

"It means, little brother, that I'm getting my dream at last."

Leila made a sound. Micah jumped to his feet, furious.

"You're going back to LA!" he yelled. "That's what you mean."

"W-well, yeah, Micah, it means—"

"I knew you would leave again!" Micah screamed, tears flooding his eyes. "I knew it!"

He bolted from the room before I could explain the situation. I started after him but Leila stopped me.

"Let me." Her voice was tight and irritated.

"I'm not leaving him! You are both coming with me, obviously."

She looked at me in disbelief.

"Obviously?" she asked skeptically. "Obviously we're coming with you?"

I felt like a steel rod had gotten jammed down my spine.

"Yes ... Obviously my brother is going with me, and I assumed—"

"You assumed I would pack up and follow you across the country without even knowing what you want from me?"

The anger bubbling from her was uncharacteristic of the woman I'd known over the last month.

"Leila, this is an opportunity of a lifetime. I thought my chance was lost but it's knocking again—at Christmas, no less."

She couldn't muster the words and instead spun and disappeared after Micah.

I gritted my teeth, tempted to follow them and make them listen, but really, what else could I say? Micah, I understood. He was a kid. He didn't know another life besides Alpena. But Leila? She should be on my side.

I slumped back onto the couch and stared blankly to the front yard. Snow started falling and I was transfixed by the neighbor's flashing lights across the street.

Christmas in LA was nothing like this. It was warm, and

bikini-clad men and women skated by on roller blades. There was no melancholy, no sense of loss.

What had I been doing involving Leila in my convoluted life in the first place? She was a simple girl with plain values. She and I were star-crossed, doomed, but I'd followed my heart and it had landed me on yet another person's hate list.

A part of me hoped she would refuse to come. It might lead to more problems. If this was how it was going to be after a month, what would it be like after a year?

But that doesn't mean I want to let her go.

The matter was solely in Leila's hands now. I could only sit back and wait for her decision, but I made one of my own in the meantime; whether or not Leila decided to come with us, I was going back to California.

10

LEILA

One Year Later

Ryan was blasting one of Jayce Joyce's singles through the stereo speakers in the living room.

"Turn that shit off right now!" I howled. My entire family looked at me in alarm but my brother hurried to oblige. No one wanted to rouse my temper, not after the last few months.

"It's not exactly Christmas music, is it?" Why did I feel the need to explain myself to them? My sentiments about Jayce and how we had left things had been made quite clear.

Or rather how he'd left me and taken my little friend with him. For a year, I'd been trying to make sense of how easy it had been for him to leave, like what we'd shared had meant nothing to him. Sure, he'd asked me to come, but as an afterthought. I had not been involved in his decision—he'd expected me to follow him like a puppy.

Why didn't I go?

It was a question I still couldn't answer. How many times had I picked up the phone to call him or opened my email to fire him a long, scathing message? I never had, nor had I responded to his endless messages.

That had been earlier, though. Jayce hadn't messaged in months, not since his voice had taken over the airways. I couldn't go anywhere without hearing him and it was maddening.

"Have something to eat, dear," Mom urged, shoving a hamburger in my face. I accepted and dug in. I couldn't remember the last time I'd eaten something hot.

"I hear H&M is hiring, Leila," Dad offered from the grill. It pained him to make the suggestion but he knew I needed a job. And he wanted to get me out of the house even though Mom insisted she was happy.

"Retail. That sounds swell."

"It's not too late to go back to school," Morris offered. I gave him the finger.

"LEILA!" my mother barked at me. I ignored her and focused on the burger again. I'd thought she was used to it by now.

Everyone else seemed to accept my personality change, for better or worse.

Mom regretted not putting up a bigger fight when I'd taken that "job" with the Jensens.

"I knew he'd be a terrible influence," she'd said more times than I cared to count. "I just knew it. This is my entire fault."

"I'm a grown woman, Mom," I'd reminded her just as often. "I can make my own decisions."

"Can you?" Was invariably the answer.

"The Jensen house is up for sale," Cat said, and my head whipped around.

"What?"

My sister nodded solemnly. I bit my tongue to keep myself from screaming.

"There's a 'For Sale' sign and Kendall Reynolds is the realtor.

He's selling it remotely from LA. He hasn't even come by after the tenants moved out last month."

No, Jayce hadn't returned, not to my knowledge anyway.

"What an asshole."

Again, my family exchanged nervous looks

He was selling Micah's house. Just when I'd thought I couldn't hate him more.

I closed my eyes and thought about the kid I'd loved as much as his brother, and wondered how he was doing.

What Jayce did wasn't fair to either of us, and I'll never forgive him. Never.

"He'll have to come back to Alpena for the final inspection and to sign the paperwork when it sells," Cat commented, and I zoned back in. She was saying it for my benefit.

"I guess so. I bet he'll expect a parade when he lands in his Sony-sponsored jet."

"Leila, when he comes, you should—" my mom began, but the ire in my face stopped her. She cleared her throat and looked toward Dad, who was still working at the kitchen grill.

"Or not," she stated.

"Maybe you can bring him a pie! That always works out well."

"Hey," Dad growled, frowning at me. "Just because you weren't savvy enough to stay away from a guy everyone knew was bad news doesn't mean it's your mother's fault."

I inhaled sharply, contrition filling my lungs.

"I know. I'm sorry, Mom."

At once, her arms were around my shoulders and she hugged me closely.

"You regret not going to LA with him and Micah, honey, but think about the life you'd have now. Think about the—"

"Mom, please. I don't want to rehash all this. My decision was best for everyone, no matter how hard it might be and no matter how you and Dad question me."

"We don't question you!" my parents chorused in harmony.

My siblings and I laughed.

I picked up the remnants of my burger and continued to chomp.

"Anyway," Cat concluded. "You should be on the lookout, in case he comes to town. Kendall promised to text me if she hears he's coming."

I nodded, chewing slowly. The bread started to taste like sawdust.

The eyes of my entire family were on me but I didn't meet anyone's gaze. I didn't want to engage in more banter on the matter.

They wouldn't go against my wishes and contact Jayce behind my back, but that didn't mean they agreed with my choice to cut him out; not when there was a kid involved.

"Oh." I sat up as I heard a noise, but my mom put her hand on my arm.

"I got this. Finish eating."

I smiled at her gratefully and dropped into my chair, but instinctively, my ears were trained on the rest of the house.

The doorbell rang and we curiously gazed at each other.

"Is Santa early?" Dad joked, moving to the door, but Morris stopped him.

"I'll get it, old man. Finish the burgers."

Dad laughed and whipped my brother with a tea towel as Morris scurried to answer as the bell chimed again.

"Impatient," I remarked.

"It's flipping cold outside, Leila," Cat chided me. "I'd be impatient too in three feet of snow."

I bet it's not snowing in California.

I had been thinking about Jayce a lot more since Thanksgiving. It marked the anniversary of the time we'd spent together.

I was playing a lot of the "what if" game.

What if Daryn hadn't called?

What if I'd gone with them?
What if I'd never slept with him?
It was the dumbest game a person can play. There were no winners and it only drove you closer to the brink, particularly when you already didn't get enough sleep.

"Uh, Lee?"

Morris reappeared in the doorway of the kitchen, looking petrified. All eyes were on him.

"What?"

"You have a visitor."

"Is it Melanie? Get rid of her, please!" I begged him in a stage whisper. "I can't buy any more Avon from her!"

He shook his head, his eyes huge. Suddenly my stomach lurched and I was on my feet.

"No ..." I said slowly. "It can't be."

"It's not Jayce," he assured me.

"Well?"

"It's his brother—Micah."

Instantly, the stress was back. I ran out of the kitchen, my family in tow.

"Micah!" He was standing in the foyer. He looked great, a lot taller, and wearing a designer coat with a faux-fur lining.

At least Jayce is taking care of him. I was filled with guilt. Jayce loved his brother.

That was never the matter. There were just ... other issues.

"Hey, Leila." He looked at me shyly and I rushed forward to embrace him heartily. He seemed surprised by my reaction but hugged me back tentatively while looking at my family, watching us from the hallway.

"Ignore them," I chirped, glancing nervously toward the stairs for a sign of my mother. "They don't get out much and forget what other people look like."

"It's really great to see you. Sorry I stopped by without calling or emailing, but my brother keeps a good eye on me and said not to bother you when I asked if we could visit."

The smile froze on my face.

Yeah. Make me into the bad guy. That's nice. Typical Jayce BS.

"You never bothered me, sweetheart ..." It seemed like he wanted to be invited in, but I couldn't take the risk.

"Listen, Micah, I would love to catch up with you but we're going out ... uh, to a family thing. Could we catch up tomorrow? How long will you be in town?"

"Until tomorrow night. Jayce needs to be back in the studio Friday morning."

I heard the sob but as I turned my head, my mother was already speaking.

"Sorry, Leila. I tried to calm her, but baby wants her mama—"

It was only then that Mom saw Micah and clamped her mouth shut as my daughter continued to wail in her arms.

Micah's face turned pale and he looked at me, astounded.

"Y-you have a baby?" he inquired. I wished the floor would open and swallow me.

"Um, yes." What else could I say? Was Micah mature enough to understand my infant daughter was his niece? Mom dropped Charlotte into my arms and I began rocking her gently.

"Oh!" he peered into Charlotte's small face and a tender smile formed on his lips. "She's cute. I didn't know you got married."

There it was. I took it and ran.

"Yup," I lied. "I got married and I had a baby."

My family exhaled collectively behind me.

"But we can talk about it tomorrow."

He nodded.

"Café Crepe on Sanford?" I suggested. "Around noon?"

That was Charlotte's naptime. He nodded and gave her a long gaze that made my heart skip. Charlotte resembled the Jensen men so much, it was impossible to ignore the thick dark hair and big brown eyes. But Micah couldn't know, could he?

"See you tomorrow," he replied, retreating to the snow.

"Hang on, Micah," Morris called. "I'll give you a ride."

He shook his head.

"No—I don't want Jayce to see you," he replied. "Good night."

I fell against the door, bundling my daughter in my arms.

"Do you think he'll say anything to Jayce?" Mom asked. By her tone, she hoped he would.

"Not a chance. He's probably not even speaking to that bastard," I replied, and stalked up the side staircase with mine and Jayce's baby.

11

JAYCE

Mari was smoking a cigarette on the patio when I drove up. I grimaced in frustration.

"Where's Micah?"

She shrugged without answering. I pushed my way past her, locking the car with my key fob.

Micah was in front of the TV as usual and barely looked at me as I entered. He'd acted particularly standoffish since we'd returned from Michigan the day before.

"Did you have dinner?" I had a fairly good idea what the answer was. I had been in the studio all day and was bone tired. The last thing I wanted was to cook. Not when I was paying Mari.

I also paid her for keeping the house. Not like it mattered—she was outside, smoking a cigarette. She appeared to be scrolling through her messages.

I would have fired her but she was the third nanny/housekeeper since returning to Cali with Micah. Easily, she was the best. The first one had smoked meth; the second had webcammed from my bedroom while Micah was at school—I'd gotten home early one day.

Neither of the three interacted with Micah. I began to think we were better off. In good conscience, I couldn't leave my eleven-year-old brother alone in LA.

The more time I spent around the women in Los Angeles, the more I missed Leila. But she'd made it clear from the day I left—if I went, we were done.

I'd thought that, in time, she would come around, but she'd ignored my emails, my texts, and my phone calls. A neighbor had said she'd moved back in with Carla but I didn't dare call there. Carla loathed me and I wasn't looking to make things worse.

The best thing to do was forget about Leila, no matter how badly it burned.

Micah didn't answer my question, so I asked again.

"Are you hungry? Did you eat?"

"No, I haven't eaten!" he barked at me. "I just said so!"

I cocked my head to the side, my own temper flaring at his tone, but he'd been acting up since we sold the house. I chalked it up to that—he was pissed at me again. I hadn't wanted to sell it, but I couldn't be a landlord from across the country. My schedule was too grueling, and no one was trustworthy enough to manage it.

Actually, that was a lie—I'd trusted Leila, but she'd flatly declined when I'd suggested it. She hadn't even wanted to stay there.

She wanted nothing to do with me.

"Get your jacket. We're going out for dinner."

He looked up from his video game with baleful eyes and rose. Of course he did—the kid loved to eat.

"Mari, we're going out for dinner," I announced as we scooted past her on the porch.

"Where are you going?" she inquired. "Can you grab something for me too?"

I pretended not to hear her as we climbed into my Audi. I was looking at a BMW, but it had to wait until after the tour.

"Do you want to tell me what's up your ass?" I asked in the way of an ice-breaker.

"You ruin everything," he spat, and I was taken aback by its swiftness.

"Can you be more specific?" I knew what was coming—he was angry about the house sale.

"You didn't deserve Leila anyway. I'm glad she's married now."

This weird sensation of both hot and cold swept through me simultaneously, and for a moment, I wasn't driving down the road. My brother's lips were moving as he spewed more venom in my direction, but I heard nothing after the opener.

"Leila is married?"

He stopped talking and shook his head, looking out the window in disgust.

"Yeah. And her kid is cute too."

That did it.

I pulled over on the side of the road so hard that the tires squealed and the car behind me laid on the horn, but I could not have cared less.

"What did you just say?"

"Yeah, you heard me. I don't think she wants you to know. I hope you're happy. We could have been a family and you fucked it up, Jason! You fuck up everything!"

It was surreal, sitting there being cursed at by an eleven year old.

"How do you know this?"

Micah scoffed.

"How do you think?" he snapped, defiantly crossing his arms over his chest. "I went to see her at her parents' house."

"The Butlers? She staying with her parents?"

"What the hell do you care, Jason? You only give a shit about your music and yourself."

He could not have been more wrong. The thought of Leila not only married but having a child with another man broke my heart into a trillion pieces. It was a punch in the gut, but explain that to a kid whose life had been turned upside down.

A burning chafed my eyes. I gritted my teeth and forced myself not cry.

So she moved on. I can't even get it up for another woman, because no one compares to her, and she's married with children. Who is this asshole she married?

It was none of my business, but I had to know.

Slamming the car in first, I did a U-turn back toward the house.

"Where are you going? I thought we were going out to eat!"

"I changed my mind. We're ordering in."

FACEBOOK. She hadn't blocked me, but we weren't friends anymore either. Her privacy settings allowed me to see her marital status.

Single.

That didn't mean a thing. Maybe she hadn't gotten around to it? Maybe she didn't use Facebook anymore?

Nah, her last public post had been three days ago. The pictures on her profile never had an unfamiliar man ... but a few depicted her pregnancy.

My mind began to run wild. I spun at the desk and stared at my brother, who was gnawing on his fourth slice of pizza.

"How old is the baby?"

He stared at me vacantly.

"What?"

"Leila's baby. How old is the baby?"

How would Micah know how old a baby was? He was still basically one himself.

"Boy or girl?"

"Girl," Micah replied, his mouth full of dough and cheese. "Charlotte."

"What did she look like?"

Micah's eyes narrowed as though he didn't quite like where the questions were going.

"Why do you care?" he asked. "She's not yours."

She better not be mine, I thought, furious at the notion that Leila had gotten pregnant with my sperm and had married another man for her daughter to have a name.

My daughter.

"What did she look like?" I asked again.

"She looked like a baby," Micah grumbled. "Kinda like me."

It was all I needed to hear, and I sprang from the chair.

"You're staying here with Mari."

"Oh, no way, Jay. Don't go bothering her! She has a life without you! Leave her alone. She's happy."

Those words caused me to freeze in my tracks, considering what he'd said.

He was right—I had no right to disrupt Leila's happiness, but she also had no right to withhold a child from me ... if Charlotte was mine.

And what if she isn't? A small, sane voice called at me. Leila wouldn't hide the fact that we had a child, would she?

My mind traveled to the day we'd parted; the hurt in her eyes when I'd chosen LA over her. There had been no sugarcoating it. She would not be there to support me along the way. And now I was missing her worse than ever.

"I-I h-have to see her, Micah," I stuttered.

How to explain the delicateness of the situation to a kid?

"You'll do whatever you want anyway," Micah shouted. "Just don't get your ass kicked by her husband!"

IF ANYONE WAS home at the Butlers, they weren't answering the door.

So I sat on the front steps, despite the freezing temperatures, going over everything in my head.

You're not here to make trouble. You're here to ask a simple question. If she's not your baby, you can walk away.

However, what to do if Charlotte was mine? I couldn't jet-set across the country with her in my arms. She was very young and couldn't be separated from her mother. Would I separate them? Would I sue for custody?

A sad realization hit me. What the heck was I doing? The Christmas melancholy struck me. Suddenly, I wanted to run away, or at least bury my head in one of the nearby snow banks.

No wonder Leila hadn't told me she was pregnant. She knew me better. I was a fly-by-night, move-on-a-whim guy who wouldn't commit to a loving woman because he was too busy focusing on himself.

I didn't deserve to be anyone's father. I couldn't even manage to be a good brother. I rose from the front steps, despair touching my soul.

Leila had done the right thing by keeping me away from my daughter, if the child was mine. She'd married someone, given her baby stability, and here I was, again, trying to wreak havoc. For all I knew, her husband thought the baby is his.

Get the hell out of here before someone sees you! It was too late. A minivan pulled into the driveway the second I unlocked my rental.

A look of disbelief colored Leila's face from the driver's seat and I dropped my head in shame. Yup, it was too late.

"Jayce! W-what are you doing here?" she gasped, almost falling out of the vehicle. She was alone but for the tiny, sleeping infant in a rear-facing car seat directly behind the passenger seat.

From where I was standing in the slush, it was impossible to tell how old she was. She could have been four months or she could have been two.

"Hi," I said weakly. She looked great. Marriage and motherhood agreed with her. Her pale skin was tinged with pink where the scarf didn't cover her face and I could see she'd gained some weight but it filled her perfectly.

"What are you doing here?" There was more firmness in her tone this time. I knew her as well as she knew me. She couldn't hide the fact she was happy to see me, even though uncertainty flashed over her face.

Now was the time for the moment of truth. Ask her about Charlotte! She was alone. Would she lie to me? I'd be able to tell.

"I came to see Charlotte."

The words just blurted out and a shadow crossed her face.

"Micah told you."

It wasn't a question.

"Is she mine, Leila? I won't make any trouble for you or your husband. I understand why you didn't tell me, why you got married so quickly, but I need to know if she's mine."

Leila didn't answer but her chin quivered, despite being so bundled against the cold. She looked away.

"I'm sorry," I told her, my voice hoarse with emotion. "I never meant to hurt you, Leila. I never realized what we had until you were gone. I don't expect you to forgive me. If you and your husband can find a way to let me into her life ... I won't make trouble, I swear—"

"I'm not married."

To say I felt relief was an understatement. My knees actually buckled, and I stumbled toward her, the sleet catching on the cuffs of my pants.

"You're not?"

She shook her head and looked back at the car where Charlotte slept.

"Your brother assumed that because of the baby, so I played along with it. I didn't want him to run back and tell you ..."

She trailed off, but she didn't have to finish her thought. I knew what she was thinking.

"Boyfriend?"

She scoffed. "Hell, no."

Was that declaration an insult or a sign of hope? I opted for the latter.

"Would you like one?" I teased, closing the small gap between us. She peered at me, and my heart skipped a beat.

"I'm not going to Los Angeles with the baby," she declared.

"I'm not asking you to. I already made the mistake of letting you go once, Leila, and I'm not doing it again."

She gazed at me, pulling the scarf down to expose her face against the cold.

"You're coming back here?"

"I'll figure something out," I hadn't thought that far ahead. "If you'll let me be in Charlotte's life ... and yours."

She was still wary, but it appeared she wanted to believe everything I was saying.

"Leila, I love you."

Her eyes widened and her lips parted in disbelief.

"Y-you do?" she choked.

"I do. From the minute you entered my life! The second I

touched down in LA without you, the greatest sense of loss overcame me. When you wouldn't take my calls or emails—"

"I wanted to give you a clean break," she interjected, and I wanted no fight with her.

"I don't blame you. You did the right thing—you always do the right thing, Leila. Since I met you, I've become a better person. Less hotheaded."

"Funny," she quipped. "Since I've met you, I've become fouler-mouthed and sullen. Just ask my family."

I had to laugh.

"May I kiss you?" I asked softly, leaning forward to brush my lips against hers. At that second, an earth-shattering wail met my ears and I jerked away.

Leila giggled.

"Get used to that," she chuckled. "Her sense of timing is uncanny."

She hurried to slide open the van door and deal with the woken child as I watched in astonishment.

She was undeniably mine. The hair, the eyes, the sulky pout—all Jensen traits.

"Charlotte," Leila cooed gently to the fussing baby once she collected her. "Meet your daddy."

Leila held her toward me and a wave of panic struck me.

"Are you sure?" I whispered. "She's so small."

Leila laughed.

"I'm sure. She's tougher than she looks."

Eagerly but tentatively, I reached for my baby daughter. Instantly, Charlotte quieted, looking up at me with curious brown eyes.

"You're tougher than you look, huh?" I breathed. "Maybe you're like your mommy."

My eyes pulled away from the baby long enough to meet Leila's blue eyes.

"Thank you," I rasped, my chest full of emotion. "For everything."

Leila smiled enigmatically.

"It's been more my pleasure than you realize," she replied. "And by the way, I love you too, Jason Jensen."

The End.

EXILE: A SINGLE FATHER & A VIRGIN ROMANCE

By Michelle Love

When single father Avery McKenna moves with his seven-year-old daughter, Hattie, to a secluded lighthouse one hundred miles from Seattle, he realizes he is ill-prepared to raise a child on his own. Hiring teacher Miro to both home-school and care for Hattie, he is drawn to the young and beautiful woman who soon becomes a best friend to his daughter. Can he risk beginning a relationship so soon after his movie star wife left him, or will he ruin Hattie's chances of happiness if the relationship goes wrong?
Miro Harper finds herself drawn to this little family, and to Avery, but will her past come back to haunt her?
When Hattie falls seriously ill, all thoughts of romance are put aside. And when Hattie's mother comes back to claim her child, will it leave their fragile little family fractured forever?

It was one hundred and eight miles from Seattle to their new home—a converted lighthouse in a remote part of Washington State. Avery tucked Hattie into the back seat of the car. Fresh snow had begun to fall as he steered the car onto the Interstate.

Avery let her ride shotgun and tried to persuade her to sleep. When that didn't work, he switched on the radio and let Hattie choose the station.

She found a station playing Christmas carols—Christmas had fallen three days ago—and left it on that. Then she and her father sang along quietly.

An hour later they had fallen silent, and Avery looked over at his daughter. Hattie was still awake, her bright eyes watching the lights of the other cars on the Interstate. Since Lydia had left him—left *them*—Hattie had been more reserved than her usual exuberant self. The divorce, so sudden and so cruel, had been a shock, and when her mother had bid them both farewell, something in Hattie had been broken. A trust. Avery loved his daughter very much but, for now, he didn't know how to reach her to comfort her.

Avery sighed. At thirty-nine, a writer for a comic book series, he'd been blindsided by Lydia's affair with one of her co-stars—then devastated by the revelation that it hadn't been the first time she had been unfaithful. Lydia McKenna's star shone bright in Hollywood, and Avery had been happy to play the faithful husband, the low-key one of the two of them. He didn't want the limelight or the fame.

Now he wondered how he could ever have been so naïve. *Damn it, Lydia, how could you do it to Hattie?* That had been his overriding thought, and when Lydia had left, she hadn't left quietly. They had been hounded by the press out of the Seattle home they had loved; even after Lydia had moved out, they never left Avery and Hattie alone, watching them like hawks, commenting on every decision Avery made—people on message boards in China, for God's sake, were telling him how to bring up his daughter.

The worst thing was that Hattie began to be bullied at school. Jealous of the attention heaped on her by the press and the teachers who tried to protect her from it during school hours, the other kids got nasty. Even some of her close friends turned on the confused girl.

"What did I do?' she asked Avery one day after a particularly nasty incident, the look of fear and confusion in her eyes breaking his heart.

So, when the opportunity to exile themselves away for a few months presented itself—a friend who lived in the converted lighthouse on the Oregon coast was travelling around Asia and needed a house-sitter—Avery asked Hattie if she would like a change. They both agreed they would.

Avery felt both relief and nervousness now as he drove along the snowy road; he still wasn't sure he was doing the right thing, but it was done now, and they had to make the best of it.

"Pa?"

He looked over at Hattie and smiled. "Yes, Bub?"

"Do you think there's a heaven?"

Avery was surprised. "Where did that come from?"

Hattie shrugged. Avery was quiet for a moment before he spoke again. "Well ... hmm. Depends on what you mean. Where you go when you die?"

"Maybe.'

"Well, I guess we'll find out one day.'

Hattie wasn't happy with that answer. "But do you think there is one? An actual place?"

"I'd like to think so; it's a nice idea, isn't it? But big pearly gates and angels? I'm not sure."

Hattie wriggled in irritation, and Avery knew he wasn't answering the question the way she wanted him to. Hattie was never a child to be fobbed off with vague answers; she had been incredibly bright from a young age, and Avery had been glad to see his daughter grow to be uninterested in Lydia's celebrity world. Instead she buried herself in books and writing, like he had done when he was a kid. Avery looked at her now.

"Look, Bub, the way I see it is this—either there is life after death, or there isn't. If there is, great, we get another chance. If not, I guess, it'll just be like being asleep, but forever, and that's gotta be relaxing, huh?" He grinned sideways at her. "Anyhoo, it's not something you'll have to worry about for a very long time."

Their song came on the radio—*I'm a Believer* by the Monkees. Avery started to sing softly. That did it. He saw Hattie's eyes start to close. He had sung this song to her ever since she was a baby—he said it reminded him of the day she was born.

"Never knew I wanted kids until I saw your face," he would say, "My whole life changed in that minute."

With Avery singing, and the warmth of the car heater in their faces, Hattie finally fell asleep. She woke as the car pulled up to the door of the lighthouse. Perched on the cliff, they could hear the roar and roil of the sea churning far below them. It was late. The temperature had dropped below freezing, and the driveway was slick.

They dumped their bags and Avery brought the little hold-all in with their night-things and wash bags. In the kitchen, which was surprisingly large, Avery heated up tomato soup and made grilled cheese sandwiches, while Hattie changed into her pajamas and yawned as she sat up at the table. They ate in silence, looking around at the unfamiliar surroundings. The lighthouse had an annex with a kitchen, the living room, and utility room.

After eating, they explored a little, despite the lateness of the hour. They climbed the stairs, past the little bedrooms built into the structure, to the lantern room at the top. Avery hugged his daughter to him in the freezing cold room. Hattie leaned back towards him.

"I'm glad we're here, Dad. Now we can start to get back to normal."

Avery's heart ached with sadness. "I'm sorry for everything, sweetheart. You didn't ask for any of this."

Hattie said nothing.

"How do you feel about living here?"

"I don't mind, Pa. I like it."

"What about moving away from your friends at school?"

She shrugged, not meeting his eyes. "I don't mind."

Avery was silent for a time. "When we get settled, we'll start looking for someone to come in and school you. I know you can do the math and science by remote learning, but I think I'd like an English tutor for you here. Would that be cool?"

"Cool," she agreed, and he grinned.

After a little while, she looked at him. "Pa? What about Mom? Will she come visit us here?"

Avery sighed.

"Bub ... your mother ... well, look. I've got to make sure we make the most of the opportunities that come along, things that would be good for us as a family. Your mother knows that. Whether she agrees or not." This last he muttered under his breath, but Hattie heard and nodded, understanding.

Avery kissed her forehead. "We'll talk some more about it soon, kiddo. Time for bed now. I'll be in to see you in a while."

Miro Harper knew the second she turned into the dark street that she had made a mistake. *Take back the night,* she had told herself when she decided to walk home from the bar, but things didn't always work out like that.

She had shoved her long dark hair into the hood of her sweatshirt and walked assertively through the damp Seattle night, but now, downtown, walking down Sixth, she wished she had taken a cab.

There were two of them, and the fact that they were obviously working together made her heart thump and her skin burn with fearful anticipation.

Fight or flight?

She didn't get a chance to do either.

When her roommate and best friend, Anna, came to visit her in the hospital, she had taken one look at Miro's bruised face and burst into tears. Miro just felt numb inside. The two men had beaten her, robbed her, and assaulted her—but, thankfully, they had not raped her.

Thankfully. Miro shook her head at that. Like being robbed and sexually assaulted wasn't equally as devastating. Like being told "Tell anyone and we'll kill you ... we know where you live" wasn't terrifying enough, knowing she'd been targeted. Like them debating whether to just kill her anyway, as she lay there bleeding and bruised, was fine.

Like having a knife pressed against her skin wasn't bad.

Miro had been released from the hospital, and then the police had advised her and Anna to change apartments; the men who attacked Miro were known to be vengeful. Four murders had already been linked to attacks like Miro's.

Anna, terrified, had quit her job and gone home to Connecticut. Miro had moved into a cheap motel while she looked for a new place.

When she saw the ad in the *Times*, she knew she had to apply.

Wanted: Professional English tutor to live in with single father and seven-year-old daughter. Must be willing to take on some caretaking duties for child and become part of the household. Appropriate salary based on experience, and free board and lodging. Please note: property is in remote location. Must be able to drive.

Miro Harper had been at the top of her college classes and was about to graduate when the terrible news came. Her parents and her younger sister had been killed in a traffic accident. Miro, the daughter of two renowned doctors, George Harper and Deanna Chu, had simply shut down. She slept walked through her graduation, watched as someone else gave the valedictorian speech she was meant to give, then moved across the country from her Harvard home to escape everything that reminded her of her family.

Anna was the only friend she had let get close to her. Anna was soft and warm and had met Miro on her first day of teacher training. They both taught at a prestigious private school in Seattle at first, but then Miro had moved to another school, in the city, in a more deprived area, wanting to make a difference.

As she was driving down to Oregon on the Interstate for her interview with Avery McKenna, she felt a spark of hope for once. Maybe this would be the new life she had been looking for, for so long. She had felt rootless and lost for so long now that she was beginning to feel she would never belong.

A quiet woman, Miro had reached twenty-four without forming any long-term romantic attachments. Maybe because she was terrified of loving someone only to lose them again ...

From the outside, no one would ever guess that the beautiful young woman with long dark hair, large chocolate-brown eyes, and a sweet smile, was still be a virgin. Miro had guarded the one thing she had control over in her life and, on the rare occasions she had dated, once the guys had realized they weren't going to get her into bed, they lost interest, despite her good looks, intelligence, and warm personality.

Miro didn't care. And the longer she waited, the less important it seemed to be rid of it. She focused on her career and had enjoyed working with the less-well-off kids, until the attack. But she wanted out of the city now and this job—*God, please let me get it*—would be perfect.

She had covered up the yellowing bruises on her face with make-up, and now, as she pulled the car up to the lighthouse, she glanced in the rearview mirror to check they were still hidden. Getting out of the car, she looked up at the building. It was austere and forbidding, to be sure, but there was something so inviting about it-the solitude, the strength.

The door opened and a small girl out came and smiled at her. Her dark curls stuck up in all directions; her smooth café-au-lait skin brought out the striking bright green of her eyes.

"Hello, you must be Miro ... I like your shirt. Pa said that if I came out to meet you first, then it might make you feel safer. Come in, please."

Miro felt a warm feeling creep into her bones; the girl was adorable, and Miro felt gratitude towards her father for his consideration. She shook the little girl's hand, and she introduced herself as Hattie.

"Not Harriet, because I hate that, just Hattie. I like your name."

"It's Chinese. Well, that's what my mom used to tell me," Miro told her. Hattie had hold of her hand and was leading her through the ground floor of the lighthouse. Miro saw the warm glow coming from a door at the end.

"We have a log fire," Hattie informed her, "because it's so cold, and we do everything in the living room at the moment. Pa usually has his own room to write in, but it's too cold at the moment."

Avery McKenna was sitting at a desk at the far end of the warm room; he stood when he saw them come in, and Miro's heart nearly failed. Tall, with dark, messy curls, and the same green eyes as his daughter, Avery Harper was one of the handsomest men she'd ever seen. His crooked smile, half-shy, half-wary, made her stomach flip. He shook her hand, his warm fingers dwarfing hers.

"Hi there. Please, come, sit. It's good of you to drive all this way out." His voice was deep and resonant, with a slight break that Miro found endearing. *Stop gaping at him like a lunatic,* she told herself, realizing her mouth was hanging open slightly.

Hattie made them both coffee as they chatted; Avery asked Miro about her teaching experience and seemed impressed when she told him she had worked with underprivileged kids. Hattie sat next to her father, and Miro could see the child scrutinizing her. Hattie was wise beyond her years, she decided, and she smiled at the girl.

"You look like the kind of girl who likes books, blanket forts, and reading past lights out. I was like that."

Hattie looked delighted, and Avery chuckled. "I think you just hit the nail on the head—although now I'm worried about the kind of influence you'd be."

Miro laughed, not taking offense. "I will admit, full disclosure, that when it comes to reading, I would *totally* be a bad influence."

Avery laughed, and Hattie tugged on her father's shirt. He looked at her, and a moment of unspoken communication passed between them. Avery put his hand on his daughter's head, then turned to Miro, hesitating for a just a second.

"Miro ... I—sorry, *we*—we would like to offer you the position."

Miro was surprised—she had figured she'd go back to Seattle and wait for his call—if he *ever* called. "Really?"

"Really."

Hattie laughed, and to everyone's surprise, launched herself onto Miro and hugged her. "I know we're going to be best friends."

Miro grinned and hugged the little girl, smiling gratefully at her father. "I know it too. Thank you so much."

Miro moved in two days later, and from the start, Avery knew he had made the right decision. Even though Miro was an English teacher, she helped Hattie out with all her lessons, handling the correspondence with the online schools and raising complaints if needed. She reported Hattie's progress back to Avery as they shared a bottle of wine after Hattie was asleep; it became a ritual before long.

Avery was able to work nearly all day, undisturbed, as Miro took care of Hattie. Once lessons were done for the day, they would hike along the cliffs or climb down the precarious stone steps to the beaches below and look for tide pools along the coast. Or Miro would drive them into the nearest small town for hot chocolate, after which they'd go haunt the local bookstore. Avery often commented that Miro must spend all of her own money on Hattie. He offered to repay her, but Miro wouldn't hear of it.

"We have a great time," she told him now, as they sat in front of the fire, a storm roiling around outside the lighthouse. "Hattie reminds me of why I wanted to be a teacher in the first place."

They talked about each other's lives, slowly confiding their pasts. Miro couldn't believe Lydia would just abandon her own child, but Avery tried to excuse his wife's behavior.

"It's a different set of rules in Hollywood," he said, "It's all about *that* person. What I mean to say is, Lydia is all about Lydia. Then, if she has time, Hattie *might* get some attention."

Miro was studying him. "What about you? Did she have any time left for you?"

Avery met her eyes. "I think the fact that we're divorced probably answers that." He held her gaze for a beat too long, and she saw the pain in them.

"I'm sorry, Avery. She's an idiot."

Avery smiled wryly and tapped his glass against hers. "She is that."

Avery was starting to look forward to these times alone with Miro. Sometimes they would talk late into the evening. He found her intelligent, funny, and smart, her natural warmth enveloping him and Hattie and bringing a sense of ... what was it? *Home*, he thought, *she felt like home.*

The day Hattie had led her into the room, something had changed in Avery's heart. This girl, fifteen years his junior, with a haunted look in her eyes, had touched him deeply, and her obvious love for Hattie was palpable.

Do not fall for your kid's teacher, he told himself sharply, but he couldn't help the way his heart would lift when he saw her wearing blue jeans and sneakers, hair messily pulled into a bun,. There was something so artless and so natural about her—the polar opposite to Lydia and her high-maintenance presence.

And he thought, maybe, Miro was feeling it too. They would talk sometimes late into the night, sitting closely on the couch, utterly relaxed in each other's company, laughing and fooling around.

Two months later, the weather changed for the better—spring was on its way, and Avery started to spend more time with his daughter and Miro. Thanks to Miro's help, and Hattie's patience, he'd been able to finish his book ahead of the deadline and was happy to be able to hang out with them both. He even sat in on a couple of Hattie's lessons and saw how well Miro was able to instruct his daughter, helping her out with math too, most of which was a foreign language to Avery. He held up a textbook in disbelief.

"When is Hattie ever going to make use of this?"

Miro grinned and looked at what he WAS indicating. Algebra. "Hey, don't underestimate Hattie—she might be an astronaut one day."

"Yeah, Dad," Hattie shot back, rolling her eyes at him. "I might be the first human on Mars."

Avery held up his hands, grinning. "My mistake. I apologize."

The two of them ganged up on him then, teasing him, and Avery laughed, feeling a sense of contentment he'd forgotten how to feel.

It was as summer was beginning that everything changed on a Saturday, on a late afternoon in June. Hattie had gone to nap, complaining of a headache. Miro sat on the counter in the kitchen, watching Avery attempting to make brownies.

"Is it self-rising or plain flour?" Avery said, his brow creasing. Miro rolled her eyes, grinning. There was a question every two minutes.

"Plain. Also, you mix the stuff in a thing called a bowl."

Avery glared at her. "You're funny. You and our kid should do a comedy routine." He didn't seem to realize what he'd said, but Miro felt her heart warm, and didn't correct him. Instead, she entertained for a long moment the fantasy that this *was* her family, her daughter ... her man. God, the tight feeling in her stomach when she imagined Avery being hers ... she knew it was wholly inappropriate to feel this way, but she couldn't deny her attraction to him.

"You have to mix it until there's no flour showing or it'll taste wrong."

"Nag."

"Doofus."

Avery laughed. "You're fired."

Miro grinned. "Again? That's the third time today. You'd starve without me." She hopped of the counter and reached for the bowl. "Just let me do it."

Avery pulled the bowl away from her. "Nah, I can do it."

Miro laughed, and tried to snatch it from his grip. Avery hid it behind his back. "You're not getting it, no way."

She reached around his waist and grasped it. "Give it up, McKenna."

She met his gaze, the atmosphere changed—God, he smelled so good—and then his lips were against hers, the bowl was forgotten, and they were kissing. It was such a natural thing, so obviously right that they both forgot themselves. Miro's arms curled themselves around his neck and Avery's hands were on her back, then cupping her face as he kissed her.

They were both breathless when they broke away. Miro started to speak, but Avery hushed her.

"Don't say anything. Just ..." He pressed his mouth to hers again, and Miro lost herself in the sweet sensations flooding her body at his touch. His arms tightened around her waist, and he murmured her name in a way that made her groin quiver with longing.

She had to tell him, though, if this was going to happen ... she had to tell him that she'd never done this before, that if she made a mistake, it wasn't him, it was *her* ... all these things spun through her head, as she felt his hands slip under her T-shirt.

"Avery ..."

But he shook his head. "It's okay ... it's okay ..."

He pulled her T-shirt gently over her head, then paused, checking to see if she was good. She smiled up at him—God, he was *beautiful*—and as he unclasped her bra and dipped his head to take her nipple into his mouth, Miro gasped, feeling herself getting wetter and hotter for this glorious man. More than that, she *wanted* to be vulnerable in his arms, and when he had stripped her, and was running his hands all over her body, Miro let herself go.

Avery picked her up and laid her down on the couch as he removed his own clothes, and she saw him naked for the first time. His broad shoulders and thickly muscled arms, so often hidden under sweaters, flexed now with his movements. His hard chest and firm stomach felt so good against her soft curves. Avery stroked the hair away from her face. "Are you sure?"

She nodded, feeling his cock hard against her thigh. *Now. Tell him now.* "Avery." Her voice was a whisper, "I've never ..."

His eyes widened in surprise. "No? Then, really, Miro, you need to be sure. We can stop, if you're not ready."

"No." she took his face between her hands. "I am ready. I think I've been ready from the first moment I saw you."

That delighted him, she could see, and he trailed the back of his fingers down her belly. "We can take this slow."

"I want you, Avery. I've never wanted anything more in my life."

His kiss was rough then, passionate, reacting to her words. His hands slipped between her legs and began to stroke her clit, gentle caresses which sent shivers through her body, and he stroked her into her first orgasm.

Miro buried her face in his shoulder to muffle her cries. "God, Avery ..."

When he had made sure she was ready for him, he slipped a condom on his huge, rigid cock, and hitched her legs around his waist.

"Darling Miro ... if you're scared, if I hurt you, we'll stop. Please don't be afraid."

But she moaned at him to hurry up, and then he was gliding his cock into her, and Miro felt only elation. It hurt a little, but she wanted him so badly that she didn't care. Moving together, their bodies entwined, Miro realized she had come home ... that here, with this man, was her place in the world.

"I love you," she said, with tears in her eyes, and Avery gazed down at her, his eyes serious as he nodded.

"As I love you, Miro Harper. You have changed our lives. *My* life."

He drove her gently to another orgasm; this time she couldn't help crying out as she peaked, but she didn't want him to stop, loving the joy on his own face as he came, feeling his body shudder at the force of his orgasm inside her.

They moved to his bedroom, Avery supporting her as her legs trembled. Then, as they lay down together, Avery covered her body with his, kissing her gently. "Stay with me all night," he whispered, "all night, my beautiful Miro."

She felt so safe, so loved in this man's arms, and wondered how she'd had a life before him, before Hattie, before this place. The rest of the world melted away.

The next morning she awoke wrapped in his arms. She studied his face while he slept, the dark lashes resting on his cheek. There was a little half-moon scar at the side of his eye, and she traced it with her finger. Avery woke and smiled at her.

"Good morning, lovely Miro."

She smiled. "Good morning. Listen, do you think I had better go back to my own room before Hattie wakes? She may not be ready to see us like this, and I'd hate to cause any problems."

Avery kissed her. "You always think of everyone's feelings;

another reason I love you. Yes, it might be for the best—but we should tell her soon. Hattie's not stupid. She already knows I, um, am sweet on you."

Miro giggled. "*Are sweet on me*?" She broke into more giggles as he rolled his eyes.

"*Her* words, not mine. She told me last week that she'd seen the way I look at you. I don't imagine she'll be ... unhappy."

Miro smiled. "I hope not. Look, I'll just go check on her."

Avery stopped her. "Wait. Before you go ..."

He kissed her again, and then their bodies curved around the other's, and they made love slowly, drinking each other in.

Afterwards, Miro slipped from the bed and went to her room to find her robe. She diverged from her path to Hattie's room to rescue her clothes from the living room. *I'm no longer a virgin,* she thought to herself in wonder. She felt ... changed, but in a good way, as if some of the walls she had built up inside her had come crashing down, only to reveal a new, better, more exciting life.

Her body ached pleasantly; her thighs and her vagina all pulsed with the hot blood that making love had sent through her veins. She felt alive in a way she hadn't since before her parents and sister had died.

She dumped her clothes back in her room, then went to Hattie's. Unusually, the drapes were still shut, and Hattie wasn't awake, her head buried in her book. Miro frowned and sat down on the side if her bed.

"Hattie?" She smoothed the girl's hair away from her hot forehead. Hattie half-opened her eyes and gave a moan, and fear spiked in Miro's heart. "Sweetheart, what is it?"

"Head hurts," Hattie mumbled, her voice so low Miro had to bend to hear her. "My eyes are sparkling."

"Your eyes?"

"It's like glitter sparkling. But every time it glitters, it hurts."

Miro bent to kiss her head. "Darling, I'm going to get your dad, and I'll get something for your pain, okay? Just hang on a sec for me."

Miro darted out of the room, fear making her feel sick. Meningitis? Migraine? She found Avery in his bathroom; his smile faded when he saw her expression.

"I think Hattie's really sick." She told him what Hattie had described, and Avery, his face pale, nodded.

They took Hattie to the emergency room in Portland. By that time, Hattie was completely listless, limp in Miro's arms as they rode in the back of the car together.

The staff at the city hospital was immediately on hand to help then. Hattie was taken for a CT scan, and Miro and Avery could only wait in the relative's room. Miro found herself clutching Avery's hand tightly as they waited.

Please, no, not Hattie, she kept thinking, and then there was anger. *No, you've already done this to me once; you're not taking her too.*

She squeezed her eyes shut to stop the tears, but they fell anyway. Avery pulled her to him, his own eyes troubled and scared, and they held each other.

Much, much later, the doctor came to see them, and the expression on his face made Miro's heart freeze.

"I'm afraid I have some troubling news, but I don't want to scare you. Hattie has what we think is a small tumor in her brain. The actual name for it is *medulloblastoma*. Now, before you get upset, we caught it early. Usually, in these cases, the child's pain is written off as just headaches and ignored until it's too late, but because you caught it as soon as symptoms began, we are confident that we can operate. But we will *have* to operate."

Avery could barely get his mouth to work. "Will she be okay, Doc?"

"I want to be honest with you entirely. Her chances of survival for this type of cancer are fifty to sixty percent. If you'd like, we can transfer Hattie to a cancer specialist, but our neurosurgeon here is one of the best in the country. I'll leave you to talk. You can see Hattie in a little while."

Miro turned to Avery and wrapped her arms around him. "I'm so sorry, Avery."

He leaned his head against hers and sighed. "I can't believe this."

She stroked his face. "We will help her get through this, I promise. Avery ... I think you need to call Lydia."

"God." Avery dropped his head into his hand, but he nodded. "I know." He looked up at her. "Miro, you should know, with Lydia ... she'll take over *everything*. She'll treat you like crap. I won't let her get away with it, I promise."

She kissed him. "I know you won't, but this is about Hattie, not me. I can ride out the Lydia storm."

He took her face in his hands. "Just remember I love you."

Avery had not been exaggerating. Lydia McKenna, in all her sleek, ebony-skinned, long-limbed elegance, swept into the hospital, ready for her performance as 'the concerned mother.'

Expecting the doctors to fawn over her as they would have done at Cedars Sinai in L.A., she was nonplussed that the doctors and nurses here, who seemed oblivious to her fame, ignored her grandstanding. Lydia barely acknowledged Miro's presence, but Miro could not have cared less. She sat by Hattie's bed quietly as Avery introduced her, then listened while Hattie's parents discussed their daughter's care.

When Hattie woke in the middle of the night, the intense pain had dimmed. The smell of antiseptic, pee, and stale food made her feel sick, and she screwed up her nose. The room was dark, and she could hear her father's quiet snores as he slept in a chair. A cool hand took her hand and she blinked, startled.

"Hattie? Darling?"

Her mother leaned forward and smiled at her. Hattie couldn't speak for a moment. A terrible disappointment tore through her. Then she immediately felt guilty.

"Mom?"

It sounded wrong, so wrong. The word stuck in her throat.

"Darling, you're in a hospital. Did Daddy tell you what's going on?"

"Where's Miro?"

Her mother was quiet, and Hattie saw her lips tighten. She pushed a few damp hairs away from her face. There were tubes coming from her arms, machines bleeping. Her head felt muzzy.

"Careful, darling, careful. You're very sick, Hattie, my love. When your father wakes up, we'll tell you what's going on."

"Where's Miro?" Hattie asked again.

Lydia made a frustrated noise. 'She's not part of this family, Harriet."

"My name is *not* Harriet."

Annoyed, Lydia turned away and prodded Avery hard in the ribs. He coughed and opened his eyes.

"Avery, your daughter is awake." Lydia's tone was snippy.

Avery ignored her barbed tone and smiled at his daughter. "Hey, sweetheart. How do you feel?"

"I'm okay. Where's Miro?"

Hattie heard her mother make a sound, and her chair squeaked as she shifted in it. Avery shot her an annoyed look before his expression cleared.

"Miro's at home at the moment. She'll be pleased to hear

you've woken up. She's not here ... well, because the hospital only allows two visitors per patient and ..."

"And, of course, it should be your mom and dad who stay with you," her mother finished in a high voice. Avery saw Hattie roll her eyes, and he grinned.

"Shall I call her?"

Hattie nodded with rather too much force, which made her groan in pain. Avery squeezed her hand again and left the room.

Hattie didn't want to look at her mother. There was an uncomfortable silence.

"Well," Lydia said, and fell quiet.

Hattie was in the hospital for just over a week. Lydia refused to give up her vigil at her bedside, enjoying the attention when the nurses finally praised her devotion to her child. Avery rolled his eyes and gave up his place to Miro a couple of times. Hattie's joy at seeing Miro did not go unnoticed—neither did Avery's obvious affection for her—and, one evening very late, Hattie heard her parents arguing in whispers outside her door.

"She's not her mother, Avery."

"At least she's *here*." Her father's voice was rigid with anger. "She's more of a mother than you know how to be."

Her mother gasped and began to cry. There was a silence. Then Avery sighed.

"Please, Lydia, stop with the crocodile tears."

Hattie's mother's sobs slowed and stopped.

"I suppose you think I enjoy being away from my child?"

"No, I ... ah jeez, Lydia ... I don't know what to think anymore. But Hattie's very fond of Miro, as am I, and whether or not you approve, she is a big part of our lives. I'm not sending her away because of one of your tantrums. Miro is part of this family whether you like it or not."

Another silence.

"Oh my God, you're *fucking* her."

Hattie's eyes widened, and she craned to hear what her father would say. She heard him sigh. "Keep your voice down, Lydia, for Christ's sake. Yes, Miro and I are in the early stages of a relationship."

Hattie, despite her pain, raised her arms in triumph, utterly delighted, but then she dropped them. Despite her mother's abandonment, Hattie still loved her; she *was* her mother. Just because she didn't want her and her father back together, making him sad, didn't mean she wanted her mother to be sad either.

"Well ... you moved on fast."

"Do you really want to compare 'moving-on-fasts'?"

"That's not fair."

"I think it is. At least we were already divorced when I fell in love with someone else."

Lydia sighed. "Look, Avery ... I'm just saying, isn't it a little quick? And *love*, really?"

"It's none of your business, Lydia, not anymore."

Lydia changed tack.

"My work is important, Avery. I'm doing this so that Hattie will grow up independent and strong and have the opportunities she deserves. She won't have to rely on a man."

Avery gave a short bark of laughter.

"I wouldn't say you rely on me, Lydia. And how does you being a Hollywood actress teach Hattie anything but superficiality and entitlement?"

"I rely on you to allow me the freedom to do what I do, Avery." Her mother's voice had taken on a new, softer tone. "Without you looking after Hattie ..."

"Okay, then. You need to see that, when you're away from her, Hattie needs someone to teach her about things I can't. What if you're away when she starts her period? When she gets her first boyfriend? There are some things a girl can't talk about with her dad. Miro is there for those things, Lydia."

When they had walked away and Hattie was alone, she lay back and stared up at the ceiling. Miro and her Dad. "Yes, Mom, love. *Really*." And she smiled.

Miro's presence in their home was non-negotiable. That's what Avery said and, after asking him what non-negotiable meant, Hattie agreed with him. Lydia wasn't pleased with the arrangement, but had little room to argue when her work called her away so often.

Still, things were tense, especially after Hattie went through the surgery to remove the tumor. Avery insisted that Lydia stay in a motel until Hattie was released, but Miro was uncomfortable with the thought that she would be seen as a usurper.

When Hattie awoke, the doctor gave them the good news; they had removed the tumor with clean margins. A course of chemo would follow, but Hattie should make a full recovery. Avery assumed Lydia would go back to Los Angeles, but she insisted on staying with them.

Lydia was an intelligent woman. Her mission now was to win her way back into her family's good graces. She became girlish, playful, and flirty, to remind Avery of the fun they had had when they were first together. She befriended Miro, asking her questions about her parents, watching her while she cooked, praising her recipes, her clothes, and her hair.

Miro took it all in with an amused air. She wasn't fooled for a moment, but she wouldn't say a bad word against Lydia in front of Avery or Hattie. For his part, Avery seem unimpressed with his ex-wife's machinations.

Hattie was the only one who resisted. She resented her mother for coming back, for ruining what had been so perfect a life of love and laughter with her father and Miro. Lydia didn't talk to Hattie about her work or include her in family discussions, like her father did. When she cooked, Hattie was banished from the kitchen; when the endless press people came to interview her about her 'family struggle,' Hattie was never allowed to disturb her.

As for Avery and Miro ... their relationship was on hold for the moment. They had come to the decision, not because of Lydia's presence, but to wholly concentrate on getting Hattie healthy. But working together so closely only made them fall deeper and deeper in love until, one night, Avery'd had enough.

When Miro came to tell him that Hattie was sleeping, he pulled her into his arms. "I can't wait any longer, Miro. I'm so in love with you. Please, let's make this official, you and I— share my life, share my bed ... we are a family."

She moved into his room after that and talked to Hattie about the two of them. Hattie—who already knew—was so excited that Miro felt a pang of sadness. She missed her own parents and her sister. Even Anna, who she had been so close to, now lived a country away.

Lydia continued her charm offensive, so much so that Miro felt slightly suffocated by her. She didn't say this to anyone, of course, not wanting to make trouble, but Lydia's constant presence began to wear on her.

It was almost Christmas before the call came from the police in Seattle. The two attackers had been caught—sadly, only after they had murdered another woman—and now the police were asking Miro to come help identify them.

They left Lydia with Hattie and traveled up to Seattle together. Miro was so grateful to Avery for his support, but when she had to walk into the identification room, her legs wobbled and she threw an uncertain glance at Avery. He took her hand.

"It's okay, sweetie."

She saw them immediately. "Number three and number five."

"You're sure."

"Positive."

As they walked out of the room, Miro felt something inside her break. Her final wall. She bent at the waist, trying to drag oxygen into her lungs. Flashbacks of the attack invaded her mind and she collapsed, sobbing, as Avery wrapped his arms around her, pressing his lips to her temple.

"It's okay, darling; it's all over now."

He took her to a restaurant on the waterfront, and they had chowder and sat talking. It was strange to be away from Hattie for so long, and Miro said so. Avery grinned.

"You know, she loves you as much as I do—perhaps not in the same way," he said with a wicked grin and she laughed.

"Avery ... my life changed when I met you, in every way."

"In Avery way," he quipped, and she groaned.

"You did *not* just make that joke."

"I did."

"It's over between us."

They both snorted with laughter, causing an older couple to glare at them. Avery took her hand. "Shall we go for a walk?"

They strolled along the waterfront piers, under the globe lamps, looking out at the lights of the houses and boats across the Bay. Avery wrapped his arms around her. "I love this city, but I don't regret moving away for a minute."

"Me either. I love our little place."

Avery kissed her. "You know, my friend's already extended his travels ... I might make an offer on the lighthouse."

Miro grinned at him. "I'll get in on that action. I have the inheritance from my parents." When he looked doubtful, she made a face. "Twenty-first century, boy, suck it up. Equals."

He laughed. "Then it's a deal. *Our* place. Hattie will be over the moon."

"I love her so much."

Avery kissed her tenderly then, his eyes soft with love. "You, me, and Hattie. That's the family I want now."

As she gazed up at him, Miro knew that from now on, she would always know where she belonged ...

The End

UNTITLED

©Copyright 2020 By Michelle Love All rights Reserved
In no way is it legal to reproduce, duplicate, or transmit any part of this document in either electronic means or in printed format. Recording of this publication is strictly prohibited and any storage of this document is not allowed unless with written permission from the publisher. All rights are reserved. Respective authors own all copyrights not held by the publisher.

ABOUT THE AUTHOR

Mrs. Love writes about smart, sexy women and the hot alpha billionaires who love them. She has found her own happily ever after with her dream husband and adorable 6 and 2 year old kids.

Currently, Michelle is hard at work on the next book in the series, and trying to stay off the Internet.

"Thank you for supporting an indie author. Anything you can do, whether it be writing a review, or even simply telling a fellow reader that you enjoyed this. Thanks

www.ingramcontent.com/pod-product-compliance
Lightning Source LLC
LaVergne TN
LVHW011718060526
838200LV00051B/2940